Rush Too Far

ALSO BY ABBI GLINES

The Rosemary Beach series

Fallen Too Far

Never Too Far

Forever Too Far

Twisted Perfection

Simple Perfection

Take a Chance

The Sea Breeze series

Breathe

Because of Low

While It Lasts

Just for Now

Sometimes It Lasts

Misbehaving

The Vincent Boys series

The Vincent Boys

The Vincent Brothers

The Existence series

Existence

Predestined

Ceaseless

Rush Too Far

A Rosemary Beach Novel

Abbi Glines

ATRIA PAPERBACK

New York • London • Toronto • Sydney • New Delhi

ATRIA PAPERBACK

A Division of Simon & Schuster, Inc.
1230 Avenue of the Americas
New York, NY 10020

First Atria Paperback edition May 2014

ATRIA PAPERBACK and colophon are trademarks of Simon & Schuster, Inc.

For information about special discounts for bulk purchases, please contact Simon & Schuster Special Sales at 1-866-506-1949 or business@simonandschuster.com.

The Simon & Schuster Speakers Bureau can bring authors to your live event. For more information or to book an event, contact the Simon & Schuster Speakers Bureau at 1-866-248-3049 or visit our website at www.simonspeakers.com.

Interior design by Dana Sloan
Cover photo by Ryan_Christensen/iStockphoto

Manufactured in the United States of America

10   9   8   7   6   5   4   3   2   1

Library of Congress Cataloging-in-Publication Data is available.

ISBN 978-1-4767-7594-4
ISBN 978-1-4767-7595-1 (ebook)

To Natasha Tomic, who first used the phrase
"Rush Crush." You've stood behind me,
made me laugh, listened to me worry, and
enjoyed more than one glass of red wine
with me. Over this past year you went from
being a supportive blogger to a real friend.

Rush Too Far

Prologue

They say that children have the purest hearts. That children don't truly hate, because they don't fully understand the emotion. They forgive and forget easily.

They say a lot of bullshit like that, because it helps them sleep at night. It makes for good, heartwarming sayings to hang on their walls and smile at as they pass by.

I know differently. Children love like no one else. They have the capacity to love more fiercely than anyone. That much is true. That much I know. Because I lived it. By the age of ten, I knew hate, and I knew love. Both all-consuming. Both life-altering. And both completely blinding.

Looking back now, I wish someone had been there to see how my mother had sown the seed of hate inside me. Inside my sister. If someone had been there to save us from the lies and bitterness she allowed to fester within us, then maybe things would have been different. For everyone involved.

I never would have acted so foolishly. It wouldn't have been my fault that a girl was left alone to take care of her ailing mother. It wouldn't have been my fault that the same girl stood at her mother's graveside, believing that the last person on earth who loved her was dead. It wouldn't have been my fault that a man had destroyed himself, his life becoming a broken, hollow shell.

But no one saved me.

No one saved us.

We believed the lies. We held on to our hate. Yet I alone destroyed an innocent girl's life.

They say you reap what you sew. That's bullshit, too. Because I should be burning in hell for my sins. I shouldn't be allowed to wake up every morning with this beautiful woman in my arms, who loves me unconditionally. I shouldn't get to hold my son and know such a pure joy.

But I do.

Because eventually, someone did save me. I didn't deserve it. Hell, more than anyone, it was my sister who needed saving. She hadn't acted on her hate. She hadn't manipulated the fate of another family, not caring about the outcome. But her bitterness still controls her, while I've been delivered. By a girl . . .

But she isn't just a girl. She is an angel. My angel. A beautiful, strong, fierce, loyal angel who entered my life in a pickup truck, carrying a gun.

Chapter One

This isn't your typical love story. It's really too completely fucked up to be charming. But when you're the bastard son of the legendary drummer from one of the most beloved rock bands in the world, you expect serious fuck-ups. It's what we're known for. Add the selfish, spoiled, self-centered mother who raised me into the mix, and the outcome isn't pretty.

There are so many places where I could start this story. In my bedroom, as I held my sister while she cried from the pain of our mother's cruel words. At the front door, as she watched, with tears streaming down her face, while my father came to take me away for the weekend, leaving her alone. Both of those things happened often, marking me forever. I hated to see her cry. Yet it was a part of my life.

We shared the same mother, but our fathers were different. Mine was a famous rocker, who brought me into his world of sex, drugs, and rock and roll every other weekend and for a month during the summers. He never forgot me. He never made excuses. He was always there. As imperfect as he was, Dean Finlay always showed up to get me. Even if he wasn't sober, he came.

Nan's father never came. She was alone when I was gone, and even though I loved being with my dad, I hated knowing she needed me. I was her parent. I was the one person she could trust to take care of her. It made me grow up quickly.

When I asked my dad to bring her along, too, he would get this sad look on his face and shake his head. "Can't, son. Wish I could, but your momma won't allow that."

He never said anything more. I just knew that if my mother wouldn't allow it, then there was no hope. So Nan was left alone. I wanted to hate someone for that, but hating my mother was hard. She was my mom. I was a kid.

So I found a place to focus my hate and resentment at the injustice of Nan's life. The man who didn't come to see her. The man whose blood ran through her veins yet didn't love her enough even to send a birthday card. He had his own family now. Nan had been to see them once.

She had forced Mom to take her to his house. She wanted to talk to him. See his face. She just knew he would love her. I think, deep down, she thought Mom hadn't told him about her. She had this fairy tale in her head that her father would realize she existed and swoop in and save her. Give her the love she so desperately sought.

His house had been smaller than ours. Much smaller. It was seven hours away in a small country town in Alabama. Nan had said it was perfect. Mom had called it pathetic. It hadn't been the house, though, that haunted Nan. Not the small white picket fence that she described to me in detail. Or the basketball hoop outside and the bicycles leaning against the garage door.

It had been the girl who opened the door. She'd had long blond hair, almost white. She had reminded Nan of a princess. Except that she'd been wearing tennis shoes with dirt on them.

Nan had never owned a pair of tennis shoes or been near dirt. The girl had smiled at her, and Nan had been momentarily enchanted. Then she'd seen the pictures on the wall behind the girl. Pictures of this girl and another girl just like this one. And a man holding both their hands. He was smiling and laughing.

He was *their* father.

This was one of the two daughters he loved. It had been obvious, even to Nan's young eyes, that he was happy in those photos. He wasn't missing the child he had left behind. The one her mother kept telling her he knew about.

All those things our mother had tried to tell her over the years that she had refused to believe suddenly fell into place. She had been telling the truth. Nan's father hadn't wanted her, because he had this life. These two beautiful, angelic daughters and a wife who looked so much like them.

Those photos on the wall had tortured Nan for years afterward. Again, I wanted to hate my mother for taking her there. For shoving the truth in her face. At least when Nan had lived in her fairy tale, she had been happier, but her innocence was lost that day. And my hate for her father and his family began to grow inside me.

They had taken from my little sister the life she deserved, a father who could love her. Those girls didn't deserve him more than Nan did. That woman he was married to used her beauty and those girls to keep him from Nan. I hated them all.

I eventually acted on that hate, but the story really starts the night Blaire Wynn walked into my house with a nervous frown and the fucking face of an angel. My worst nightmare . . .

◇

I had told Nan I didn't want people over that night, but she'd invited them anyway. My little sister didn't take no for an answer ever. Leaning back on the couch, I stretched my legs out in front of me and took a drink of my beer. I needed to hang around here long enough to make sure things weren't going to get out of hand. Nan's friends were younger than mine. They got a little rowdy sometimes. But I put up with it because it made her happy.

Mom running off to fucking Paris with her new husband, Nan's still-inattentive father, hadn't helped Nan's mood lately. This was all I could think of to cheer her up. For once in her life, I wished my mother would think of someone other than herself.

"Rush, meet Blaire. I believe she might belong to you. I found her outside looking a little lost." Grant's voice broke into my thoughts. I looked up at my stepbrother and then at the girl standing beside him. I'd seen that face before. It was older, but I recognized it.

Shit.

She was one of them. I hadn't known their names, but I'd remembered there were two of them. This one was . . . Blaire. I cut my eyes toward Nan to see her standing not too far away with a scowl on her face. This wasn't going to be good. Did Grant not realize who this girl was?

"Is that so?" I asked, racking my brain for some way to get her out of here—and fast. Nan was going to blow any minute. I studied the girl who had been a source of pain for my sister most of her life. She was gorgeous. Her heart-shaped face was highlighted by a pair of big blue eyes with the longest natural eyelashes I'd ever seen. Silky platinum-blond curls brushed against a pair of really nice tits that she was showing off in a tight tank top. Damn. Yeah, she needed to go. "She's cute, but she's young. Can't say she's mine."

The girl flinched. If I hadn't been watching her so closely, I would have missed it. The lost expression on her face didn't add up. She'd walked into this house knowing she was in unwelcome territory. Why did she look so innocent?

"Oh, she's yours, all right. Seeing as her daddy has run off to Paris with your momma for the next few weeks, I'd say this one now belongs to you. I'd gladly offer her a room at my place if you want. That is, if she promises to leave her deadly weapon in the truck." Grant was finding this amusing. The dick. He knew who she was, all right. He loved the fact that this was upsetting Nan. Grant would do anything to piss Nan off.

"That doesn't make her mine," I replied. She needed to take the hint and leave.

Grant cleared his throat. "You're kidding, right?"

I took a swig of my beer, then leveled my gaze at Grant. I wasn't in the mood for his and Nan's drama. This was taking it too far. Even for him. The girl had to go.

She appeared to be ready to run. This wasn't what she'd been expecting. Had she really thought her dear ol' dad would be here, waiting for her? That story sounded like bullshit. She'd lived with the man for fourteen years. I had known him for three years, and I knew he was a piece of shit.

"I got a house full of guests tonight, and my bed's already full," I informed her, then looked back at my brother. "I think it's best if we let her go find a hotel until I can get in touch with her *daddy*."

Blaire reached for the suitcase that Grant was holding. "He's right. I should go. This was a very bad idea," she said with a hitch in her voice. Grant didn't let the suitcase go easily. She tugged hard to get it out of his grasp. I could see the unshed tears in her eyes, and it tugged at my conscience. Was there something I was missing here? Did she really expect us to open our arms wide for her?

Blaire hurried to the exit. I watched the gleeful look stretch over Nan's face as Blaire walked past her.

"Leaving so soon?" Nan asked her. Blaire didn't respond.

"You're a heartless fuck. You know that?" Grant snarled beside me.

I wasn't in the mood to deal with him. Nan strutted over to us with a triumphant grin. She'd enjoyed that. I understood why. Blaire was a reminder of all that Nan had missed out on while growing up.

"She looks exactly like I remember her. Pale and plain," Nan purred, sinking down beside me on the couch.

Grant snorted. "You're as blind as you are mean. You may hate her, but she's mouthwatering."

"Don't start," I warned Grant. Nan might appear happy, but I knew that if she dwelled on it too much, she'd break down.

"If you don't go after her, I will. And I'm gonna put her sexy ass up at my place. She isn't what you two assume she is. I talked to her. She hasn't got a clue. That dumb-ass father of yours told her to come here. No one is that good of a liar," Grant said as he glared at Nan.

"Dad would never have told her to come to Rush's. She came here because she's a mooch. She smelled money. Did you see what she was wearing?" Nan scrunched up her nose in disgust.

Grant chuckled. "Hell, yeah, I saw what she was wearing. Why do you think I want to get her back to my place so bad? She's smoking hot, Nan. I don't give a shit what you say. The girl is innocent, lost, and smoking damn hot."

Grant turned and headed for the door. He was going after her. I couldn't let him do that. He was easily fooled. I agreed that the girl was easy on the eyes, but he was thinking with his dick.

"Stop. I'll go after her," I said, standing up.

"What?" Nan asked in a horrified voice.

Grant stepped back and let me pass him. I didn't turn back and acknowledge my sister. Grant was right. I needed to see if this was an act or if she really had been told by her douchebag father to come here. Not to mention that I wanted to get a look at her without an audience.

Chapter Two

She was walking up to an old, beat-up truck when I opened the door and stepped outside. I paused a moment, wondering if it was hers or if someone had brought her here. Grant hadn't mentioned anyone else. I squinted against the dark to see if I could make out someone inside the truck, but I couldn't tell from this far away.

Blaire jerked open the driver's-side door and then paused to take a deep breath. It was almost dramatic, or at least it would have been had she known she was being watched. But from the way her shoulders sagged in defeat before she climbed up into the truck, I knew she had no idea that she had an audience.

But then again, maybe she did. I knew nothing about this girl. I only knew that her father was a fucking mooch. He took what my mother and Nan gave him, yet he never returned their tokens of affection or love. The man was cold. I had seen it in his eyes. He cared nothing for Nan or my stupid mother. He was using them both.

The girl was beautiful. There was no question about that. But she had also been raised by that man. She could be a master manipulator. Using her beauty to get what she wanted and not caring whom she hurt along the way.

I walked down the steps and toward the truck. She was still sitting there, and I wanted her gone before Grant came out and fell for this act of hers. He'd take her home with him. And she'd use him until she was bored. I wasn't just protecting my sister; I was protecting my brother from her, too. Grant was an easy target.

She turned, and her eyes collided with mine before she let out a scream. Her red-rimmed eyes sure looked like she'd been crying real tears. No one was out here to see her, so there was the slight possibility that this wasn't part of an elaborate scam.

I waited for her to do something other than stare at me like I was the stranger when *she* was on *my* property. As if she'd read my mind, she swung her gaze back to her steering wheel and made a move to crank the truck.

Nothing.

She started to become frantic in her attempts to get the truck to crank, but from the click I'd heard, I guessed there wasn't a drop of gas in her tank. Maybe she was desperate. I still didn't trust her.

The sight of her hitting her steering wheel in frustration was funny. What good was that gonna do if the idiot had run her tank completely empty?

She finally opened the door to the truck and looked up at me. If she wasn't as damn innocent as she looked, then the girl was a hell of an actress.

"Problems?" I asked.

The look on her face said she didn't want to tell me that she couldn't leave. I reminded myself again that this was Abe Wynn's daughter. The one he had raised. The one he had abandoned Nan for all those years. I would not feel sorry for her.

"I'm out of gas," she said with a soft voice.

No shit. If I let her go back inside, I was going to have to deal with Nan. If I didn't, Grant would take care of her. And then she would more than likely take advantage of him.

"How old are you?" I asked. I should have known this already, but damn, I thought she was older than she looked. The big-eyed, scared look on her face made her seem so young. The way she filled out that tank top and jeans was the only sign that she was at least legal.

"Nineteen," she replied.

"Really?" I asked, not sure I believed her.

"Yes. Really." The annoyed frown was cute. Dammit. I didn't want to think she was cute. She was a fucking complication I didn't need.

"Sorry. You just look younger," I said with a smirk. Then I let my gaze travel down her body. I didn't need her thinking I was someone she could trust. I wasn't. I never would be. "I take that back. Your body looks every bit of nineteen. It's that face of yours that looks so fresh and young. You don't wear makeup?"

She didn't get offended, but her frown grew. Not my desired effect. "I'm out of gas. I have twenty dollars to my name. My *father* has run off and left me after telling me he'd help me get back on my feet. Trust me, he was the *last* person I wanted to ask for help. No, I don't wear makeup. I have bigger problems than looking pretty. Now, are you going to call the police or a tow truck? If I get a choice, I prefer the police."

Had she really just suggested I call the police? And was that disdain for her dear ol' dad that I heard in her voice? I was pretty damn sure it was. Maybe he hadn't been the model father that Nan had imagined in her head from the one short visit she'd made to that house when she was a kid. Sounded like Abe was on her shit list.

"I don't like your father, and judging from the tone in your voice, neither do you," I said, letting the idea that maybe she was another casualty of Abe Wynn sink in. He'd abandoned Nan, and it sure as hell sounded like he had abandoned this daughter, too. I was about to do something I would regret. "There is one room that is empty tonight. It will be until my mom gets home. I don't keep her maid around when she isn't here—Henrietta only stops by to clean once a week while Mom is on vacation. You can have her bedroom under the stairs. It's small, but it's got a bed."

The look of disbelief and relief on her face almost made the idea of facing Nan worth it. Even though I was pretty damn sure Blaire and Nan had father-abandonment issues in common, I knew Nan would never accept that. She was determined to hate someone, and Blaire was going to take the brunt of her anger.

"My only other option is this truck. I can assure you that what you're offering is much better. Thank you," she said tightly.

Fuck. Had I really been about to leave this girl in a truck? That was dangerous. "Where's your suitcase?" I asked, wanting to get this over with and talk to Nan.

Blaire closed the truck door and walked back to get her suitcase. There was no way her little body was picking that up and lifting it over the bed of the truck. I reached behind her and grabbed it.

She spun around, and the astonished look on her face

made me grin. I winked at her. "I can carry your bag. I'm not that big of an ass."

"Thank you a-again," she said with a stutter, as those big, innocent-looking eyes locked with mine.

Damn, her eyelashes were long. I didn't see girls without their makeup often. Blaire's natural beauty was startling. I would have to remind myself that she was nothing but trouble. That and keep my fucking distance. Maybe I should have let her get her own bag. At least if she thought I was an asshole, she'd stay away.

"Ah, good, you stopped her. I was giving you five minutes and then coming out here to make sure you hadn't completely run her off," Grant said, snapping me out of whatever trance this girl had put me under. Motherfucker, I had to stop this shit now.

"She's gonna take Henrietta's room until I can get in touch with her father and figure something out," I replied, and shoved the luggage at Grant. "Here, you take her to her room. I have company to get back to."

I didn't glance back at her, nor did I make eye contact with Grant. I needed distance. And I needed to talk to Nan. She wasn't going to be happy, but there was no way in hell I was letting that girl sleep in her truck. She would draw attention. She was gorgeous and completely unable to take care of herself. Dammit! Why had I gone and pulled Abe Wynn into our life? He was causing all this shit.

Nan was standing at the door with her arms crossed over her chest, glaring at me. I wanted her pissed. As long as she was mad at me, she wouldn't cry. I didn't deal well when she cried. I'd been the one trying to ease her pain since she was little. When Nan cried, I immediately started trying to fix things.

"Why is she still here?" Nan snapped, looking over my shoulder before I could shut the door and block out the fact that Grant was headed this way with Blaire.

"We need to talk." I grabbed her arm and pulled her away from the door and toward the stairs. "Upstairs. If you're gonna yell, I don't want to cause a scene," I told her, making sure to use my stern voice.

She frowned and stomped up the stairs like a five-year-old.

I followed her up, hoping she would get far enough away from the front door before it opened. I didn't take a deep breath until she was stalking into the bedroom she had used back when this was our summer home. Before I became an adult and took what was mine.

"You're buying her shit, aren't you? Grant talked you into it! I knew I should have followed him out there. He is such a dickhead. He's only doing this to get to me," she spat out before I could say anything.

"She's staying in the room under the fucking stairs. It isn't like I'm putting her up here. And she's only staying until I can get a hold of Abe and figure out what to do. She has no gas in her truck and no money to get a hotel room. You want to be mad at somebody, fine, be mad at motherfucking Abe!" I hadn't meant to raise my voice, but the more I thought about Abe running off to Paris knowing that his daughter was headed here in a beat-up old truck with no money, the more it pissed me off. Anything could have happened to her. She was too damn breakable and needy.

"You think she's hot. I saw the look in your eyes. I'm not stupid. That's all this is," Nan said, before sticking out her lip in a pout. "Seeing her hurts me, Rush. You know that. She had him for sixteen years. It's my turn!"

I shook my head in disbelief. She thought she had Abe now? Really? He was off living it up in Paris on my mother's dime, and Nan thought that meant she had won? "He's a fucking loser, Nan. She had his ass for sixteen years. I don't think that means she won something. He let her come here thinking he would help her and didn't think twice about the fact that she's a little helpless girl with these big-ass sad eyes that any man could take advantage of." I stopped talking, because I was saying too much.

Nan's eyes went wide. "Holy hell! Don't you fuck her! You hear me? Do not fuck her! She leaves as soon as you can kick her out. I do not want her here."

Talking to my sister was like talking to a wall. She was so stubborn. I wasn't doing this anymore. She could make all the demands she wanted, but I owned this house. I owned her condo. I owned everything in her life. I was in control. Not her.

"Go back down to your party and your friends. I'm going to bed. Let me handle this the way it needs to be handled," I said, then turned and headed for the door.

"But you're gonna fuck her, aren't you?" Nan asked from behind me.

I wanted her to stop saying that word in relation to Blaire, because, damn it all to hell, it was making me think about all that white-blond hair on my pillow and those eyes looking up at me as she climaxed. I didn't answer Nan. I wasn't going to fuck Blaire Wynn. I was going to keep as far away from her as possible. But Nan wasn't going to order me around, either. I made my own choices.

Chapter Three

The music was loudly pumping downstairs, but I knew I wouldn't be able to hear it up in my room. I wasn't in the mood for all that shit down there. I hadn't been in the mood before Blaire Wynn showed up, and I sure wasn't in the mood now.

"There you are," a female cooed, and I turned to see one of Nan's friends from the club walking toward me. Her skirt was so short her ass almost hung out of the back. That had been the only reason I noticed her. Hard to miss an ass right there on display. I couldn't remember her name, though.

"You lost?" I asked, not liking that she'd come upstairs. My rule was to keep the party away from my personal space.

She pushed her chest out and bit down on her bottom lip before batting her eyelashes at me. Long fake eyelashes. Nothing like Blaire's. Fuck me. Why was I thinking about Blaire?

"I'm exactly where I want to be. With you," she said in a husky whisper, before pressing her tits to my chest and running her hand down to cup my dick. "I've heard how good you can make a girl feel. How you can make her scream from orgasms, over and over again," she said, gently squeezing me. "Make me come, Rush."

I reached down and grabbed a strand of her blond hair. It

wasn't as blond as . . . no. Goddammit, I was doing it again. Comparing everything about her to Blaire. This was an issue I needed to get control of—now. "Beg," I told her.

"Please, Rush," she quickly replied, and she rubbed my uninterested cock to life. "I want you to fuck me, please."

She was good. Sounded almost like a porn star. "It's just sex, babe. Nothing more. And it's just tonight," I told her. I always made sure they knew the rules. We wouldn't have a repeat unless she was damn good.

"Hmm, I'll remind you that you said that," she said, winking up at me like she didn't believe me at all. Either she was fucking brilliant in the sack, or it was wishful thinking on her part. I hardly ever went back for seconds. "Where's your room?" she asked, pressing a kiss to my chest.

"Not taking you to my room," I told her, and shoved her back until she stumbled into the guest bedroom I used for sex. Girls didn't get to go to my room. That was my place, and I didn't want memories of females up there.

"Oh, Mr. Impatient," she said, giggling as she shimmied out of her skirt and licked her lips. "I'm a pro at sucking cock."

I pulled my shirt off and went over to sit on the bed. "Show me," I replied.

The smell of perfume hit my nose, and I squinted against the sun, cursing whoever hadn't closed the damn curtains last night. I rolled over, and the naked body beside me made a noise. She'd stayed all night. Shit. I hated the ones who didn't leave. They were the clingy ones. The ones who thought this was more than a fuck. Did she really think getting on her knees and sucking me off without telling me her name was going to win her points?

I stood up and found my jeans, then jerked them on. The girl yawned, and I decided I'd forgo the shirt and get the hell out while I had time. She'd get the hint when I was nowhere to be found. I opened the door slowly, slipped out into the hallway, and headed for the stairs. If I went to my room, she'd come knocking on my door. I could take off down the beach and get in a morning run. But first, I needed coffee.

I fixed a cup quickly, then headed toward the French doors leading outside. The moment I reached the door, I spotted her. That long, silky hair of hers was blowing in the breeze as she stood on my porch looking out at the water. I loved that view. It was peaceful. I wondered what she was thinking. Did she worry that Abe might not come back? Was she really going to find a way to leave? Or was she the mooch her father was?

After a night of sex with a nameless friend of my sister's, I wondered what it would be like to get close to Blaire. She wouldn't throw herself at me, and she sure as hell wouldn't get on her knees and suck me off because I told her to. Why the fuck did the idea of innocence appeal to me? That was complicated. I didn't do complicated. I couldn't ignore her, though. Not this morning. I needed to see her face again and see if that sincere look was still there. Was she angry about sleeping under the stairs? Would the claws come out now?

"That view never gets old," I said, causing her to spin around and gape at me.

I had startled her. I started to laugh when her gaze traveled down my bare chest and focused on my abs. What the hell? She was checking me out. Maybe she wasn't that innocent. The idea made my stomach sour.

"Are you enjoying the view?" I asked, masking my disappointment with amusement. She blinked rapidly as if waking from a trance and lifted her gaze back to my face. I hated the idea of her throwing herself at me. I didn't want her to be like the others. Why the fuck it mattered, I didn't know, but it did. "Don't let me interrupt you. I was enjoying it myself," I told her, unable to keep the annoyance out of my voice. I took a sip of my coffee. Her face turned bright red, and she spun around to face the water again. Why did the simple fact that she'd been caught looking and gotten embarrassed make me so fucking happy? Damn. I couldn't keep from laughing with relief.

"There you are. I missed you in bed this morning." I recognized the voice from last night. Shit. I'd wasted time, and she'd found me. Blaire turned back to look at me, and then her eyes went to the girl pressing up against me. This was good. She needed to see what a sorry-ass piece of shit I could be. This was what I wanted. She'd stay away from me if she saw this. But the flash of interest in Blaire's eyes as the girl ran her fingernails down my chest did things to me I didn't want to admit.

"It's time for you to go," I said, moving her hand off of me and pointing in the general direction of the front door.

"What?" she asked with surprise in her voice, as if I hadn't told her last night that this wasn't happening again.

"You got what you came here for, babe. You wanted me between your legs. You got it. Now I'm done," I reminded her.

"You're kidding me!" she replied with an angry snarl. Maybe she hadn't believed me last night. Her mistake.

I shook my head at my own stupidity and took another drink of my coffee. One day, I would learn that these hookups with a sleepover were trouble.

"You are not going to do this to me. Last night was amazing. You know it," she said in a whiny voice as she reached for my arm, which I pulled out of her grasp. It wasn't "Beg Rush" time anymore. We did that last night. It was fun. She got off more times than she could count. But for me, it was mediocre.

"I warned you last night, when you came to me begging and taking off your clothes, that all it would only ever be was one night of sex. Nothing more," I said, annoyed that I even had to remind her.

I didn't look back at her. I kept my eyes on the water and drank my coffee as if she'd already left. With a dramatic stomp of her feet, she left.

The horrified look on Blaire's face made me quickly get over the interruption of last night's mistake. "So how did you sleep last night?" I asked. It had to be cramped in that room, plus the stairs and the noise in the house probably sucked. This was her chance to complain. Show her true colors.

"Do you do that often?" she asked with an annoyed look on her face. That was adorable . . . dammit.

"What? Ask people if they slept well?" I wasn't going to let that face get to me. She was leaving as soon as I talked to Abe. This was his problem, not mine. The fact that I enjoyed looking at her was even more of a reason to get her the hell out of here.

"Have sex with girls and then throw them out like trash,"

she replied. Those big eyes of hers went wide, as if she were shocked at the words that had come out of her own mouth.

I wanted to laugh. She made it hard to stay focused. I set my cup down and stretched out on the lounge chair beside me. The best course of action was to get Blaire to hate me. I'd be doing us both a favor. If she hated me, I could easily keep my distance. "Do you always stick your nose where it doesn't belong?" I asked.

Instead of the anger I expected to flash in her eyes, I saw remorse. Really? I had been an ass. She wasn't supposed to look as if she were sorry for calling me out on my shit.

"Not normally, no. I'm sorry," she said with an apologetic half-smile, and she hurried inside.

What the fuck? Had she just really apologized to me? Where did this girl come from? Women didn't act like her. Had no one taught her not to back down from bullies?

I stood up and turned to look inside and found her picking up empty bottles and garbage littered all over the place from last night. I hated a mess, but I tried to overlook it when Nan wanted to party.

"You don't have to do that. Henrietta will be here tomorrow," I said, hating to see her clean up.

She put the bottles in with the trash she had collected and glanced back at me. "I just thought I'd help out."

I was calling her father this morning. I needed to get her out of here. Until then, I had to make sure she hated me. "I already have a housekeeper. I'm not looking to hire another one, if that is what you're thinking." The harsh tone in my own voice made me want to wince, but I kept the bored look on my face. I had perfected it years ago. I could not look at her right now.

"No. I know that. I was just trying to be helpful. You let me sleep in your house last night." Her voice was soft and pleading, as if she needed me to believe her. Fuck that.

We needed to set some ground rules before I fucked up. "About that. We need to talk."

"OK," she said in a whisper. Dammit, why did she look so defeated again? I hadn't kicked her damn puppy.

"I don't like your father. He's a mooch. My mother always tends to find men like him. It's her talent. But I'm thinking you may already know this about him. Which makes me curious. Why did you come to him for help if you knew what he was like?" I needed her to tell me something real. Or I needed to catch her in a lie. I couldn't keep her here much longer. Those fucking long legs of hers and her big blue eyes were driving me crazy.

"My mother just passed away. She had cancer. Three years' worth of treatments add up. The only thing we owned was the house my grandmother left us. I had to sell the house and everything else to pay off all my mother's medical bills. I haven't seen my dad since he walked out on us five years ago. But he's the only family I have left. I had no one else to ask for help. I need a place to stay until I can find a job and get a few paychecks. Then I'll get my own place. I never intended to be around long. I knew my dad wouldn't want me here." She paused and laughed, but it wasn't real. It was filled with pain, which only twisted my gut. "Although I never expected him to run off before I arrived."

Holy fucking hell. I was going to kill Abe Wynn. The moth-erfucker had abandoned his daughter while she took care of her ill mother? What kind of sick monster did that shit? I couldn't kick her out. I was, however, about to make Abe's life a living hell. The asshole was going to pay for this. "I'm sorry to hear about your mom," I managed to say through the blood boiling in my veins. "That's got to be rough. You said she was sick for three years. So since you were sixteen?" She'd been a kid. He'd left her, and she'd just been a kid.

She simply nodded and watched me cautiously.

"You're planning on getting a job and a place of your own," I said, wanting to remind myself that this was her plan. I could help her long enough so that she could achieve this. Some-one needed to help her, dammit. She was fucking alone. "The room under the stairs is yours for one month. You should be able to find a job and get enough money together to find an apartment. Destin isn't too far from here, and the cost of living is more affordable there. If our parents return before that time, I expect your father will be able to help you out."

She let out a small sigh, and her shoulders sagged. "Thank you."

I couldn't look at her. It made me want to murder Abe with my bare hands. Right now, I couldn't focus on Nan and her need for a father. The man she wanted as a father was a bastard. A bastard I was gonna make pay for this shit. "I've got some things to do. Good luck on the job hunt," I said, before walking away from her. I had a phone call to make.

Chapter Four

I let the phone ring three times before hanging up and dialing again. I would call my mother's phone until she answered. She'd better not fuck with me, or I would turn the damn thing off and cancel her credit cards. She'd be calling me then.

"Honestly, Rush, is it really necessary to call me incessantly? If I don't answer, leave a message, and I will return your calls when it's convenient for me."

"I don't give a shit about your convenience. I want to talk to the motherfucker you're married to. Now."

Mom huffed into the phone. "I most certainly will not listen to my son talk to me that way, or to my husband. You can call back when you're ready to speak with respect and—"

"Mom, so help me God, if you don't put that man on the phone, your phone and credit cards will be shut down within the next ten minutes. Do not fuck with me."

That shut her up. Her sharp inhalation was the only response I got.

"Now, Mom," I repeated firmly.

There was muffled whispering before I heard Abe clear his throat. "Hello," he said, as if he wasn't ignoring the fact that he had abandoned his daughter.

"Understand one thing. I control it all. The money. My

mother. Everything. It's mine. You fuck with me, and you will be cut off. I brought you here because I love my sister. But you're showing me that you're not worth her time. Now, explain to me how you told your other daughter to come to my house and then just left the motherfucking country."

Abe paused, and I heard him take a deep breath. "I forgot she was coming."

The fuck he did. "She's here now, dipshit, and she needs help. You and my mother need to get on a plane and get your asses back here."

"I haven't seen her in five years. I don't . . . I don't know what to say to her. She's an adult now. She can make her own way. I shouldn't have told her to come to your house, but I needed to tell her something. She was begging for help. If you don't want her there, then send her away. She's a smart girl. She has a gun. She'll survive. She's a survivor."

She's a survivor. Had he just said that? For real? My head started throbbing, and I pressed my fingers against my temples for some relief. "You have got to be kidding me," I managed to say through my complete, horrified shock. "She just lost her mother, you sorry piece of shit. She's fucking helpless. Have you seen her? She's too damn innocent to be walking around unprotected. You can't tell me she's a survivor, because the girl who showed up on my doorstep last night looked completely broken and alone."

The hitch in his breathing was the only sign I had that he gave one shit about his daughter. "I can't help her. I can't even help myself."

That was it. He was refusing to come home and do anything about this. Blaire was left here for me to either help or throw out. He didn't care. I couldn't form words. I ended the call and dropped the phone to the sofa before staring out the window in front of me.

Nan had hated this girl most of her life. She had envied her. Blamed her. For what? Having a father worse than the mother we'd been given?

There had been no knock on the door leading to the top floor, which I claimed completely. I heard the door open, followed by the sound of footsteps. Only one person would walk up here without knocking.

"I put gas in her truck," Grant said as his foot hit the top step. "You don't have to pay me back."

I didn't look back at the guy I considered my brother. We had been stepbrothers once, when our parents had been married for a short time. I'd needed someone to lean on at that point in my life, and Grant had been that someone. It had bonded us.

"You gonna keep her under the stairs like Harry fucking Potter?" Grant asked as he plopped down onto the sofa across from me.

"She's safer under the stairs," I replied, cutting my eyes in his direction. "Far away from me."

Grant chuckled and lifted his feet to rest on the ottoman in front of him. "Knew you couldn't ignore the fact that she was smoking hot. That innocent, big-eyed thing she has going for her is even more tempting."

"Stay away from her," I told him. Grant wasn't any better for her. We were both fucked up. And she needed security. We didn't have that to give to her.

Grant winked and leaned his head back to stare up at the

ceiling. "Calm down. I'm not touching her. She's the kind you admire from afar. I can't promise not to admire, though. 'Cause damn, she's fine."

"Her mom is dead," I said, still unable to believe Abe had known her mother was sick all this time and had done nothing.

Grant dropped his feet to the floor and leaned forward to look at me, resting his elbows on his knees. The concerned frown on his face only reminded me how tenderhearted my brother could be. I couldn't let him make a mistake and hurt Blaire. He wouldn't mean to, but he would, eventually. "Dead? Like recently?" he asked.

I nodded. "Yeah. She's alone. She came here because Abe told her he'd help her get on her feet. Then he left."

Grant let out an angry hiss between his teeth. "Motherfucker."

I agreed with him. Completely.

"Have you talked to Abe?"

Before my conversation with Abe, I had disliked him and had been disgusted with him. Now I hated him. I hated that I had brought him here. That I had let his selfish, cold heart into this family. There was no one to blame but me. "He said he can't help her," I replied. The distaste in my voice was obvious.

"You're gonna help her, though, right?" Grant asked.

I wanted to yell that this wasn't my problem. That I hadn't asked for this shit. But I had—when I'd brought that man into this house. "I'll make sure she gets a job that pays well and is safe. When she has enough money to get her own place, I'll do what I can to help her find something affordable."

Grant let out a sigh of relief. "Good. I mean, I knew you would, but it's good to hear you say it." Only Grant expected me to do the right thing. Everyone else saw me as a rock legend's spoiled son. Grant saw more. He always had. Not letting him down was one of the reasons I did something with my life. I didn't become what the world assumed I would. Or what many thought I was. I had made my own way because someone believed in me.

"Best place for her is the club," I said, reaching for my phone. I was a member of the Kerrington Country Club, which was the hub of this small tourist town of Rosemary Beach. A job there would be safe for Blaire, and it would pay her well.

"Don't call Woods. He's a dick. He'll take one look at her and make it his goal to fuck her," Grant said.

The idea of Woods Kerrington, son of the club owner, touching Blaire made my skin crawl. Woods was a nice guy— we'd been friends most of my life—but he loved women. He loved them for one night, and then he was done with them. I wasn't judging—I was the exact same way. I just didn't intend to let Woods touch Blaire. "He won't touch her. I'll make sure of that," I said, before calling the human-resources director of the club.

Blaire had already found the club, and Darla had already given her a job. I couldn't help but grin. Maybe she was tougher than she looked. But the small tug of pride I felt for her stopped my suddenly good mood. Why the hell was I smiling like an ass because Blaire Wynn had gotten herself a job? So what?

She was nineteen, not ten. I wasn't supposed to feel anything toward her. She was a fucking stranger. One I had despised most of my life.

I reached for my phone and called Anya. She was always available, and she always left when we were finished. She didn't sleep over. It was the only reason I brought her back over and over again. That and the fact that she gave the world's best head and made some killer Italian food.

She would get Blaire out of my mind. And Blaire would come home and see me with Anya tonight. Not that Blaire needed reminding to stay away from me. She was terrified of me. The only time I had seen interest in her eyes had been that morning when she'd turned to see me watching her. She had more than enjoyed seeing me without my shirt on. Problem was, I fucking loved it.

Yeah . . . I was calling Anya. A fuck with a no-strings-attached, dark-haired beauty was exactly what I needed.

Chapter Five

She had watched me. Fuck.

It had been so easy to close my eyes and sink into Anya while picturing Blaire's face looking up at me. Her mouth slightly open and her cheeks pink. The fast breaths she would take as I filled her over and over again. I'd come so fucking hard I had been weak when it was over.

I also hadn't been able to look at Anya. I had felt like an ass. I didn't fuck women while picturing someone else in my head. It was wrong. But I had felt Blaire watching me. My entire body had come alive when the heat from her gaze found me.

When I had turned my head just enough to glance back at her, the door to the pantry was closing behind her. She had left. But her presence had made me harder than I'd ever been. Why was she getting to me like this?

The first thing I noticed when I walked into the kitchen this morning was that the place was cleaned up. I hadn't left it like this. I had sent Anya home with a peck on the cheek and a thanks, before closing the door on her and running off to my room to pace and curse.

Which meant . . . Blaire had cleaned up. Why was she cleaning shit up? I told her I didn't need her to clean up.

I moved to make coffee, slamming cabinets and drawers as

I went. I hated thinking of Blaire in here cleaning up the mess Anya and I had made. I hated the fact that she'd done it after watching me fuck Anya. But more than those things, I hated the fact that I gave a fucking shit.

"Who the hell pissed in your Wheaties?" Grant's voice startled me, causing me to slosh scalding-hot coffee on my hand.

"Stop fucking sneaking up on me," I growled.

"I knocked on the damn door when I walked in. What's your deal?" Grant sounded as unfazed by my angry outburst as I expected. He went behind me to fix himself a cup of coffee.

"You made me burn my hand, you dickwad," I snarled, still pissed that I had been so lost in my thoughts that I hadn't even heard Grant enter the house.

"No coffee yet, huh? Drink up. You're acting like an ass. After your night with Anya and her talented oral skills, I would have thought you would be in a much better mood."

I stuck my hand under the cold tap water in an attempt to cool off my heated skin. "I just woke up. And how did you know Anya was here last night?"

Grant jumped up and sat on the counter before taking a sip of coffee. I dried my hand on a towel and waited for him to tell me how he knew about Anya.

"She called me last night. Wanted to know who the girl was living in your house." He shrugged and took another sip.

I wasn't sure I liked the sound of this. How did she know about Blaire? I hadn't told her.

"Stop with that confused frowning thing you do. It's annoying," Grant said, waving his cup in my direction with a smirk. "She saw Blaire last night when she came home. Apparently, you two were getting busy outside, but she saw Blaire over your shoulder. She was curious about why she disappeared under your stairs . . ." he said, trailing off.

I could tell there was more to the story, so I waited. When Grant didn't continue, I glared at him.

He chuckled in response, then shrugged. "Fine. I was going to leave out the part where you looked back at Blaire and then fucked the hell out of Anya. She noticed something switched in you, dude. Sorry, but you're not that good at covering your emotions up." His grin grew wider. "Best fuck she's ever had, though. But then, she hasn't had me."

I was gonna have to send her flowers. Or something. Shit! She had known it was Blaire that got me off last night. I was an even bigger dickhead than I thought.

"It's Anya. She doesn't care. You know that. She's in it for the sex, just like you are. Nothing more. But I will suggest that you get your shit together, and fast. If Blaire is getting under your skin, then you need to stop it. Now. She's not an Anya, and you know it. Besides, you can't touch her. She is gonna hate you when all this comes out. Her dad, your sister, all of it. You can't go there, and you know it."

He was right. Blaire was not someone I could ever get close to. Soon I would be her enemy, and she'd hate me as much as I had hated her over the years. The only difference would be that she had a reason to hate me. I would deserve her hate. "I know," I said, hating the way it tasted on my tongue. The truth.

"I've got to get to work. Thought I'd come by and let you know about my late-night call from Anya first, though," Grant said, jumping down and carrying his cup to the sink.

"Thanks," I said.

He slapped me on the back. "It's what I'm here for. To

keep your stupid ass straight," he teased, and then turned and walked away.

I waited until the door closed behind him before heading to the shower. I had a full day ahead. First, I needed to send some flowers and an apology card to Anya. That would be the end of our fuck visits. I couldn't do that to her now. Even if she was cool with it, I wasn't.

Nan was waiting for me when I walked back downstairs after getting dressed. I was wondering how long she would stay away pouting. She knew Blaire was here, and she was pissed. Her long red hair was gathered to the side in a ponytail that fell over her bare left shoulder. The white tennis skirt she was wearing was meant to be worn with a matching polo. But that was too boring for Nan. She had ordered a tank top that she had some fancy name for. I had made fun of her for weeks.

"She's still here," Nan said in an annoyed tone.

"No, she's at work," I replied, knowing that wasn't what she meant.

"Work? She's at work? You've got to be kidding me!" Nan's tone went from annoyed to a screech. My little sister wasn't used to not getting her way with me. I was the one person in the world who moved mountains to make sure she was happy. But this time . . . this time, it was different. I wasn't hurting someone innocent just to make Nan happy. I had my lines, and she'd pushed me to draw one here.

"Nope," I said, walking past her and toward the living room, where I was sure I'd left my wallet last night before getting naked outside.

"Why is she working? Why is she still here? Did you call Mom?"

Nan wasn't taking the hint. She was going to make me tell her that I wasn't giving in this time. She was going to lose this argument with me. I wasn't kicking Blaire out. Not for her . . . hell, not for anyone. The girl needed help. "She got a job. She needs money to get on her own feet. Her mother died, Nan. She buried her mother alone. All fucking alone. Now the father you two share is off in Paris with our mother, enjoying life. I'm not just throwing her out. This is my fault."

Nan stalked toward me and grabbed my arm tightly. "Your fault? How is this your fault, Rush? She's no one to us. *No one*. Her mother died, but I don't care. Her mother ruined my life. So that sucks for her. But none of that is your fault. Stop trying to save the world, Rush."

I had created this heartless woman. Another thing that was my fault. Nan had been neglected as a child, and I had tried like hell to make up for it. Instead, I'd created a heartless, vengeful adult. I would do anything to change that, but I didn't know how.

I looked down at her and wished I didn't still see the sad little girl I wanted to save. It would make it so much easier to be hard on her. But she was my baby sister. She always would be. I loved her for better or for worse. She was my family.

"It's all my fault. Blaire's problems and yours," I said, and jerked my arm free of her hold. I grabbed my wallet off the coffee table and headed for the door. I had to get away from my sister. She wasn't helping my mood.

"Where is she working?" Nan asked.

Pausing at the door, I decided that was something Nan would eventually find out herself, but I wouldn't tell her. Blaire needed more time to settle in before my sister went after her.

I would see what I could do to be there when that happened. "Don't know," I lied. "Go visit your friends. Go play tennis. Go shopping. Just go do what it is you do that makes you happy. Forget about Blaire being here. She's my problem, not yours. Trust me to do this right."

I opened the door and left her before she could say anything else. I was done with this conversation. I had shit to fix.

Chapter Six

A text from Anya said that two dozen yellow roses weren't necessary. That was it. Nothing more. I knew it was the clean-cut end to our occasional fucks. My guilt eased where she was concerned, as I stuck my phone back into my pocket and continued running.

I ran when I needed to think and clear my head. I also ran when I'd had too many drinks the night before. Tonight I just needed to run. I didn't want to be home when Blaire walked inside. I didn't want to face her. I didn't want to hear her voice. I just wanted distance.

She deserved my help. But that was it. I didn't want to get to know her. I sure as hell didn't want to be her friend. The day she left, I would be able to breathe easy again. Maybe go visit my dad. Get away from here and enjoy life a little.

But then, fate had a way of laughing at my plans.

I slowed down as my eyes adjusted to the darkness, and I easily made out the silhouette of Blaire in the moonlight. Fuck me.

She didn't see me . . . yet. She was staring out at the water. Her long blond hair was blowing back off her face and dancing around her shoulders. The moonlight made the color of her silky strands look silver.

Her head turned, and those eyes of hers locked with mine. Shit.

I should have just nodded at her and run up to the house. Not said anything. Just kept going. I was letting her live here; I didn't have to speak to her. But damn, I wasn't going to be able to help doing that.

I stopped in front of her and watched as her gaze focused on my chest. The fact that I was suddenly glad that I was shirtless wasn't good. I shouldn't care that she was staring at my chest like she wanted a lick. Fuck. Fuck. *No!* She didn't want to lick my chest. Where the hell had that idea come from? She was fucking with my head. Dammit. I needed to get her eyes off my body. Now.

"You're back," I said, breaking the silence and snapping her out of her thoughts.

"I just got off work," she replied, lifting her gaze back to my face.

"So you got a job?" I asked, needing to keep her attention on my face.

"Yes. Yesterday."

"Where at?" I already knew the answer, but I wanted to hear how she had gotten it. What she was doing and if she liked it. Wait . . . was she wearing makeup? Holy hell, she had mascara on. Those eyelashes could actually get longer.

"Kerrington Country Club," she said.

I was unable to stop looking at her eyes. They were amazing without fucking makeup. But damn, with just a little, they were unreal. I slipped my hand under her chin and tilted her head up so I could get a better look. "You're wearing mascara," I said, as explanation for my strange behavior.

"Yes, I am," she said, moving her head so that she was free of my touch. I let my hand fall away. I shouldn't have touched her. She was right to stop that. I had no right to touch her like that.

"It makes you look more your age," I said, taking a step back and looking down at her uniform.

I knew that uniform well. I had slept with more cart girls over the years than I wanted to admit. It was the reason I had picked up golf in my teen years. Once the college-age cart girls found out who my daddy was, they were very interested in taking me for a ride in their carts. In many ways.

"You're the cart girl at the golf course," I said, lifting my eyes to look back at her. I already knew that, but seeing her in the uniform made me smile. She wore it well.

"How did you know?"

"The outfit. Tight little white shorts and polo shirts. It's the uniform. You're making a fucking killing, aren't you?" It wasn't really a question; it was a statement.

She shrugged, then straightened her shoulders, moving back a little more from me. She sensed the need to keep her distance from me. Good girl. She might be tougher than I thought. "You will be relieved to know that I'll be out of here in less than a month."

I should have been relieved. Hell, I fucking wished that was what I was feeling right then. It would mean I had one fewer problem. But I liked her here. I liked knowing I could keep her safe. Or that I was doing something to make up for the wrong I'd done to her already. Unable to stop myself, I took a step toward her. "I probably should be. Relieved, that is. Real fucking relieved. But I'm not. I'm not relieved, Blaire."

I leaned down until my mouth was just a breath away from her ear. "Why is that?" I asked in a whisper, before inhaling her sweet, clean smell. Would she smell like this between her legs? Would she be as sweet and fresh? A new kind of sweat broke out on my body, and I moved back. I was getting off track. "Keep your distance from me, Blaire. You don't want to get too close. Last night . . ." Fuck, why was I talking about this with her? I needed to forget it had happened. "Last night is haunting me. Knowing you were watching. It drives me crazy. So stay away. I'm doing my best to stay away from you," I said in a harsh tone meant for myself more than anything. But I couldn't explain that to her. I just turned and ran. I had to get away.

Once I was safe in my room upstairs, I went to the window and stared down at the beach below. Blaire was still there. But she wasn't watching the waves this time. She was looking back at the house. What was she thinking? Had I scared the shit out of her? Or was she waiting for me to change my mind and come back? I reached up and touched the cool glass with my palm and watched her. It seemed like forever and not nearly long enough before she walked back to the house.

That night, I dreamed of her for the first time. Vivid images of her underneath me. Both of her long legs were wrapped around me, and her head was thrown back as I brought her to a release we both felt.

I was so fucked.

Chapter Seven

Rush!" Jace called out from his perch on a bar stool as I walked into the club. This wasn't normally my scene, but when I'd gotten three texts from people telling me that everyone was meeting up here tonight, I decided the distraction was needed.

"Finlay's here," someone else called out. I headed for the bar, and Jace slid a shot toward me as I approached him. Jace was Woods Kerrington's best friend. He was a good guy. I just wouldn't call us close. I wasn't close to anyone other than Grant. He was the only one I trusted.

"Drink up," Jace said, smiling. The blonde on his arm looked familiar, but Rosemary Beach wasn't a big place. I'd probably been with her at some time myself.

"Hey, Rush," the girl said with a flirty smile, and I realized I did know her. Couldn't remember her name, though.

I nodded and threw back the tequila. I wasn't much for shots, but if I was going to have to endure this place, I needed to have a few shots of something.

"You lost?" Grant asked with a chuckle as he walked up beside me.

I smirked. "Probably," I replied. "Are you?"

He glanced back over his shoulder. "No. I'm here because of Nan."

Frowning, I followed his gaze and saw Nan stumbling around and laughing loudly while some guy I didn't know held on to her barely clothed body. "What the fuck?" I had started to move around him when he grabbed my arm.

"Don't. She likes him. They're dating. But she's been drinking a little too heavily lately. Thought I'd come check on her, and this is what I found. Just stand back and watch. If either of us does something too soon, she'll leave with the dick, and we'll both be dealing with more drama than we want."

He was right. Nan was an adult. I wasn't her daddy, and I needed to let her make her own mistakes. Clearing her path was exhausting, and it wasn't helping her. "You ask around about him?" I said.

Grant put a beer in my hand. "Let's go sit and wait. I think she's fine. He's Charles Kellar, Old Morrison's grandson. Goes to Harvard. Here visiting his grandparents this week."

At least he was her age. I took a drink of the beer and watched as Nan pulled the guy out to the dance floor and kicked off her spiked heels. At least she wouldn't break her damn ankle.

"She's not taking the Blaire thing well, is she?" Grant asked.

I shrugged. I wanted not to give a shit that Nan was upset. She needed to grow the fuck up and realize she wasn't the only person on the planet. But I couldn't *not* care. "No. But she needs to accept it. It's not like I'm sleeping with Blaire. I'm just giving her a place to stay," I replied.

"But you wanna sleep with her," Grant said, grinning.

"Shut up," I snarled, and shot him a warning glance.

"Damn, Rush, *I* want to sleep with her. No, I take that back. I want to fuck her gorgeous brains out. She's—"

I was out of my seat and in his face so fast I surprised myself. "Don't!" I yelled. I took a deep breath to get control of the sudden anger boiling inside me. "Stay away from her. Do. You. Understand. Me."

Grant didn't shrink back or nod in fear of pissing me off. Instead, my brother chuckled. "Holy fuck," he muttered, and shook his head. "She's gotten to you."

That had me backing up and shaking my head. He didn't know what he was talking about. I just didn't like someone helpless and sweet being talked about like that.

"Rush, I didn't think you'd come t'night," Nan slurred as she sauntered up to our table and grabbed the empty stool in front of her to steady herself. "You've met Charles? Or no? I can't remember," she said, and pulled herself up to sit on the stool.

"No, I haven't," I replied, glad for the interruption, even if it was a drunk Nan.

"Charles Kellar," the guy said, holding out his hand. "Are you Rush . . . Finlay?" he asked, his eyes going a little wide as he said my last name with an almost reverent tone. He was a fan of my father's. I knew that look.

I nodded and took a drink of my beer while ignoring his hand. I wasn't shaking the fucker's hand. I knew his kind. He'd found out Nan's connection to Slacker Demon and managed to squeeze his way into her good graces. Stupid shit didn't realize he was one of many. I'd been down this road before. A sober Nan would have spotted this bullshit right away.

"He's a big fan of Dean's," Nan said, rolling her eyes and

waving her hand toward Foster. "I already know. He's using me to meet you, and I'm using him because he's a really good fuck," she said way too loudly.

Grant was out of his seat and moving before I could say anything. "I got her," he told me. I nodded in his direction before looking back at Foster. Nan squealed and fussed at Grant, but he used his charming ways to soothe her as he moved her toward the exit.

"I don't take well to douchebags using my sister. You do yourself a favor and stay the fuck away from her. I like your grandparents, but I don't give a fuck who they are. Don't fuck with my family. Understood?" I kept my tone low and even, as Foster's eyes went wide and he nodded. Slamming down my beer, I stood up and followed the same route Grant had taken with Nan earlier.

Grant's truck was gone when I finally made it to the parking lot. He was taking Nan home. I didn't have to call him to check on that. I headed for my car and decided it was safe to go home now. Blaire should be in bed. I wouldn't have to see her.

The relief I felt at seeing her beat-up truck safely parked in the driveway was something I wasn't in the mood to admit right then. Yes, I was getting obsessive over her safety, but that was because I was a fucking protector. My mother had forced that role on me at a young age, and it was in my damn blood now. I couldn't help it. Nothing more.

If we were lucky, Blaire would be asleep.

Chapter Eight

Two days had passed since I'd seen Blaire. Avoiding her hadn't been easy. Fighting the urge to come downstairs and see her every morning was hard. But that wasn't why I was breaking my rule today. At least that was what I was telling myself.

Grant had shown up drunk with one of his regular girls. I didn't know if they would be up early, but I didn't want Blaire encountering them in the kitchen. To be perfectly honest, I didn't want her getting the wrong idea if the girl was there alone. She'd already made her feelings about my sex life very clear. I should have let her think this was another one of my hookups . . . but I was heading downstairs anyway. Unable to stop myself.

"Did you just come out of the pantry?" the girl, whose name I couldn't remember, was asking Blaire in a confused tone. I took longer strides, needing to get into that damn kitchen and shut the girl up. Blaire didn't have to answer to her.

"Yes. Did you just come out of Rush's bed?" Blaire asked. Her soft voice curled around the words, making the question seem innocent. I slowed down, surprised to detect a territorial undertone.

"No. Not that I wouldn't get into his bed if he'd let me,

but don't tell Grant that. Never mind. He probably already knows," the girl said.

I stopped at the doorway and searched the kitchen for Blaire. She was standing on the other side of the island. The girl was between us, hindering my view.

"So you just got out of Grant's bed?" Blaire asked. I bit back a smile. The confusion in her voice sounded awfully like relief to me.

"Yep. Or at least, his old bed."

"His old bed?" Blaire asked.

I fought the urge to remain and listen to just how far Blaire would go with her questioning. I fucking liked it. She gave a shit, and I liked it. Damn, this was bad.

The girl moved, and Blaire's eyes shifted until they locked with mine. I was caught. Conversation over. Time to fix what was becoming an issue. Me dealing with interest in Blaire was one thing; her having interest in me was another. She knew nothing. I couldn't let her like me. Not even a little. In the end, she'd hate me, and I never needed to know what it felt like to have her feel anything other than lack of interest toward me.

"Please, don't let me stop you, Blaire. Continue to give Grant's guest the third degree. I'm sure he won't mind," I told her, as I leaned against the doorway and acted as if I were getting comfortable.

Blaire's eyes went wide before she ducked her head and dusted crumbs off her hands into the garbage can. I had never actually seen her eat. I was glad to see signs that she was eating.

"Good morning, Rush. Thanks for letting us crash here last

night. Grant drank entirely too much to drive all the way back to his place," the girl said.

"Grant knows he has a room when he wants it," I said, without looking at the girl. I kept my eyes on Blaire, then made my way over to the island.

"Well, uh, I guess I'll run back upstairs, then." The girl was still talking, but I ignored her. She wasn't of any consequence to me. I'd prefer it if she left. When I heard her footsteps fade away down the hall, I closed the distance between Blaire and me.

"Curiosity killed the kitty, sweet Blaire," I told her, loving the way her cheeks turned pink. "Did you think I'd had another sleepover? Hmmm? Trying to decide if she had been in my bed all night?" Fuck, I wanted to touch her. She was shifting nervously, but for just one goddamn minute, I wanted to feel her close to me. *No!* I had to remember who she was. What I'd done. That keeping her away from me would save us both in the end. "Who I sleep with isn't your business. Haven't we gone over this before?" She was supposed to be angry with me. She wasn't supposed to be looking at me with those big, defenseless eyes. Unable to keep my hands off her, I reached over and wrapped a lock of her hair around my finger. The silky texture made me tremble slightly. I was getting too close. This was wrong, and it was dangerous. "You don't want to know me. You may think you do, but you don't. I promise."

If she would just see that, this would be easier. But instead of running from me, she kept looking at me like there was something more here. Something other than an arrogant asshole. How the fuck was she seeing through the persona I was projecting for her? She wasn't supposed to see anything other than the spoiled brat the world assumed I was.

"You aren't what I expected. I wish you were. It'd be so much easier," I whispered, realizing I had said it out loud. Dropping her hair, I stepped back, then turned and left the kitchen. I needed to stay away from her. But how the fuck could I do that with her in my house?

◈

It had taken me hours to finally fall asleep, only to be woken up by my phone ringing. Rolling over, I grabbed my cell phone off my nightstand and squinted against the light of the screen. It was Will. My little cousin. Shit. Not again.

"What?" I snarled into the phone, already knowing why he was calling. He had either run away again and was on his way to my house, or he was already at my house and needed to get inside. My mother's sister was a bitch. A raging bitch. I understood that completely, but the kid couldn't keep running away. Especially to here.

"I'm outside," he said.

"Shit, Will. What is it this time?" I asked, throwing the covers back and searching for a pair of discarded sweats to pull on.

"She's making me go to camp. All fucking summer," he replied. "In Ireland!"

Which translated into: she wanted a summer free of the burden of motherhood and was getting ready to ship him off. It would probably be the best summer of his life. A summer free of her.

I ended the call and threw the phone down before making my way downstairs to the front door. Opening it, I winced at the sight of Will holding an overnight bag as if I would actually let him move in. I had raised one kid; I wasn't raising another.

"You're going home in the morning. You will fucking love Ireland. Go to Grant's room for the night. Sleep there," I grumbled, closing the door behind him.

"I don't even speak Irish," he complained.

How the fuck had this kid made it to high school? "They speak English, you dipshit," I said, slapping him on the back of the head. "I'm exhausted. You woke me up. Now, go the fuck to sleep."

He nodded and slumped as if I had just ended his world. I ignored the pouting and followed him up the stairs. This wasn't a first for us. Will ran away to my place whenever I was nearby. His mother liked to visit Rosemary Beach in the summers, so it happened most often then.

"You ever been to Ireland?" he asked, as he reached the door to the room he would be crashing in for the night.

"Yep. Gorgeous country. Now, go to sleep," I replied, then headed back up to bed.

He was going home tomorrow, but I'd have to call Grant to come get him. As soon as I got to my aunt's and he started fighting with her, I would cave and bring him back here with me.

Grant would be able to take him home. He had done it for me more than once.

Chapter Nine

My bedroom door slammed, and I sat up in bed, rubbing my face and trying to block out the sunlight.

"He's back home," Grant announced.

"Thanks," I muttered. I had texted Grant last night about Will's appearance and asked if he'd take Will home before he went to work that morning.

"Little shit is a handful. He tried to take Blaire home with him." Grant chuckled.

At the sound of her name, I dropped my hand and looked at him. "She still here?" I asked.

Grant nodded his head toward the windows. "Out there. In a fucking bikini. I may stay here all day instead of going to work, if you don't mind. Besides, you owe me one for taking Will home and dealing with the evil witch."

I grabbed my discarded sweats and yanked them on quickly before walking over to the window.

Miles and miles of empty beach stretched just beyond my front yard. Blaire was lying out there with her eyes closed and her face tilted toward the sunshine. Yeah . . . Grant's ass was going to work. He wasn't staying here to sit around and stare at her all day.

"She's gonna burn," Grant said in a hushed whisper, and I

tore my gaze off Blaire to see him staring down at her just as reverently as I was. Fuck that.

"Don't look," I snapped, and moved back from the window.

Grant let out a laugh. "What the hell does that mean, 'Don't look'?"

It meant not to fucking look. "I don't . . . just . . . you remember who she is. She'll hate us, and she'll leave soon. So don't." I wasn't sure what I was saying. I just wanted him to stop looking at her. She was barely covered up, and all her smooth skin was right there for anyone to see. I didn't want anyone to see it.

"She won't hate us, just you. And Nan. And her father. But I didn't do shit," Grant said.

My hands clenched into fists at my sides, and I closed my eyes and took a deep breath. He was doing this on purpose. He wanted to see if I reacted to her. He was trying to piss me off. "Don't you have work to do?" I asked calmly.

Grant glanced back at the window and shrugged. "Dude, I work for my dad. I'm the boss. I can take off when an emergency comes up. Besides, aren't we celebrating Nan's birthday tonight?"

He was baiting me. Reminding myself of that, I walked over to the closet and found a pair of board shorts. I was going out there. She might not be wearing sunblock, and she needed it. Her skin would burn. I would hate for her to burn her skin.

"You going for a swim?" Grant asked teasingly.

I didn't look back at him. "Go to work, Grant. Nan's party is tonight," I replied, and slammed the bathroom door behind me. I had forgotten that I was giving Nan a party for her birthday tonight. Blaire was making me forget everything.

"You're playing with fire, man. Like massive flames that will eat you up! Should've let me have her. This ain't gonna be pretty," he called out loudly enough that I could hear him through the door.

"You don't know what the fuck you're talking about. No one gets her. She'll be leaving soon," I yelled back.

Grant's laugh faded away as he left my room. He was right. This was fire, and I couldn't seem to get away from it. I kept moving closer, knowing it was going to consume me if I wasn't careful.

I didn't think about what I was doing. I just changed and headed outside to check on her. "Please tell me you have sunblock on," I said as I sank down onto the sand beside her.

She covered her eyes from the sun before opening them and looking over at me. She didn't respond. Had I woken her up?

"You are wearing sunblock, aren't you?" I asked.

She nodded and pulled herself into a sitting position on the small bath towel she was using. Her body was distracting as hell.

"Good. I'd hate to see that smooth, creamy skin turn pink," I replied before I could stop myself.

"I, uh, put some on before I came out here."

I really should have looked away from her, but that seemed impossible at the moment. The tops of her breasts were right there, swelling over her bikini top. If she were anyone else, I would have no problem reaching over and tugging the small piece of fabric down until I could see her nipple. Then I'd . . . *no!* Dammit. I needed to focus on something else.

"You not working today?" I asked.

"It's my day off."

"How's the job going?"

This time, she didn't reply right away. I watched her as she stared up at me. She wasn't paying attention to my words so much as she was studying my face. I liked that. Too damn much. "Uh, what?" she asked as her face turned slightly pink.

"How is the job going?" I asked again. I wasn't able to keep the amusement out of my voice.

She sat up straighter and tried to look less interested in me. "It's going good. I like it."

The guys who no doubt flirted with her and gave her ridiculous tips annoyed me. "I bet you do," I said.

"What is that supposed to mean?" she asked.

I let my gaze travel down her body slowly. "You know what you look like, Blaire. Not to mention that damn sweet smile of yours. The male golfers are paying you well."

She didn't get angry or snap at me. Instead, she looked surprised. I turned my attention to the water. I didn't need to look at her. She distracted me. I forgot about everything else when I was focused on her. Remembering why she was here and that I'd had a hand in her pain should have made it easy enough to stay focused. But she made me forget everything. One bat of her eyelashes, and I was lost.

I had been so damn stupid back then. Asking Abe why he was so willing to leave his family of sixteen years for a daughter he had ignored for even longer would have made sense. But I hadn't asked him. I had just been thankful when he showed up. But the asshole had left a broken family behind. A young girl alone to take care of her mother.

"How long ago did your mom pass away?" I asked her. I

suddenly needed to know how long she had been struggling alone. It wasn't like I could fix it now. I just wanted to know.

"Thirty-six days ago," she murmured.

Fuck. She'd lost her mother a little more than a month ago. She hadn't even had a chance to mourn. "Did your dad know she was sick?" I asked. I would kill him. Someone needed to make the bastard pay. He hurt everything he touched.

"Yes. He knew. I also called him the day she passed away. He didn't answer. I left a message."

I had never hated anyone the way I hated Abe Wynn at that moment. "Do you hate him?" I asked. She should. Hell, I hated him enough for both of us. When I beat his face in, I would do it for her. For her mother. And I wasn't sure I would be able to stop.

"Sometimes," she said.

I hadn't expected the truth. Admitting that you hated your father couldn't be easy. Unable to stop myself, I reached over and slipped my pinkie around hers. I couldn't hold her hand. That was too much. Too intimate. But I had to do something. She needed some reassurance that she wasn't alone. Even if I was the last person on earth who deserved to be there for her, I was going to be the one. I just had to find a way to do it and fix this hell I'd created.

"I'm having a party tonight. It's Nan, my sister's, birthday. I always give her a party. It may not be your scene, but you're invited to attend if you want to."

"You have a sister?"

I thought she knew that already, but when I thought back to the night Blaire had arrived, I realized that Nan had kept her distance and hadn't actually met Blaire. "Yeah," I replied.

"Grant said you were an only child," she said, watching me carefully.

Grant had talked to her about me. He didn't need me to explain anything to her. I wanted to protect her from the truth. I moved my hand away from her. "Grant really has no business telling you my business. No matter how damn bad he wants in your panties," I said, before turning and walking back to the house. Why had I let that get to me? Dammit.

Chapter Ten

Nan had hired a party planner. I stood at the top of the stairs and watched as the decorating crew hauled in white roses by the truckload. Did she think this was her wedding? What the hell?

"I don't want to know what this party is costing you. Here," Grant said, as he walked up behind me and shoved a glass of what smelled and looked like bourbon into my hand. "Drink it. You're gonna need it."

I took a long drink and let the smoothness of the liquor coat my throat. It didn't make the fact that I was about to be faced with all of Nan's friends any easier. Normally, when she had parties here, I limited the people she could invite. Tonight I had given her no limits. I was dreading that. All of fucking Rosemary Beach was likely to show up.

"The princess has ordered roses, I see," Grant said, amused, as he leaned against the banister and watched the activity below.

"It seems that way," I said. I was still pissed at him for talking to Blaire about me. I knew he wouldn't tell her anything she didn't need to know, but it still bothered me.

"Did you invite Blaire?" Grant asked, trying to sound casual.

"Did you expect me to make her hide under the stairs all night?" I replied. Because, honestly, I had thought about it. Inviting her to this damn thing only meant I had to watch her closely. Guys would be all over her, and girls would be vicious. She needed protection from both.

"Well, I wasn't really sure. This is Nan's party," he reminded me, as if I needed reminding.

"It's at my house," I said, shooting him an annoyed glare.

Grant chuckled and shook his head. "Damn. Never thought I'd see you put someone else before Nan."

"Don't," I warned him. "Don't go there. I'm just being nice. Nothing more."

Grant cocked an eyebrow, which he knew annoyed me. "Really?"

I slammed my glass down on the railing and walked back to my room. I wasn't in the mood to watch any more of this or listen to Grant. It was going to be a long night.

One would think that Nan was the daughter of royalty, the way my house looked once the decorators were through. I moved through the rooms, keeping my eyes on the kitchen and, when I could, the pantry door. I hadn't seen Blaire the rest of the day, but I knew she was here. I'd watched her while she'd lain out on the beach long after I'd left. I'd watched her swim in the waves and then take a walk. Hell, I'd even watched her read a book.

When she had finally picked up her towel and headed back to the house, I had stood up from my relaxed position on the sofa facing the wall of windows and went to get ready for tonight. I had wanted to make sure I was down here when she came out of her room for the party.

The party was getting packed, and the music was getting louder. Still no sign of Blaire. I wondered if she was scared to walk out into this. Should I let her stay tucked away in her room safely? Or did I need to go get her?

"I'll keep my eyes on the pantry door while you go outside and get some blond surfer dude off the damn railing before he falls to his death," Grant said in my ear, before shoving me toward the balcony.

Damn drunk college kids.

I went outside and found Jace already pulling the guy down off the ledge. "Dude, go drink some coffee," Jace said with disgust, and slapped him hard on the back.

"You know him?" I asked.

Jace shook his head. "No. Just wasn't in the mood to watch anyone die tonight," he replied, before taking a drink of beer.

"Thanks," I said.

Anya walked up and wrapped her arms around Jace's waist, smiling at me. Seemed she had moved on. Good for her.

"Anya," I said, nodding a greeting in her direction.

"Rush," she replied with a teasing grin.

"And I'm Jace," he said loudly over the noise. "As much as I love fun and awkwardness, I think we'll go on out for a little walk on the beach," he said, before leading Anya toward the stairs that led down to the sand.

I headed back inside and toward the kitchen. I was going to get Blaire out of that damn room. She didn't need to stay there all night.

"She already came out," Grant said, walking up beside me. "Woods has her in the foyer."

"Woods?"

"Yeah, dude. Kerrington. Surely you've figured out that by now, he's spotted her on the course. He plays a shit ton of golf."

I shoved past the people in front of me and headed for the foyer.

The shy smile on Blaire's face, looking up at Woods as he led her into the living room, stopped me in my tracks. Someone was talking to me, but I couldn't focus on what they were saying. The blush on Blaire's cheeks had my complete attention. Woods's hand touched her back in a possessive way, which bothered me. How well did she know Woods? Had I missed this completely? Blaire said something to Woods, and he stopped to look down at her. They were discussing something. Then he leaned in close to her, and my annoyance instantly transformed into being pissed off.

Blaire's eyes shifted and locked with mine. They went wide with surprise, as if she didn't expect to see me at my own house. Then she moved away from Woods and spoke to him quickly as she put more distance between them. She was saying something to him, but he seemed amused and ready to say whatever he needed to in order to get her to stay.

I knew exactly the kind of guy Woods was, because he was just like me. I wasn't letting him touch her. He saw her as a conquest, and I would kill him before I let him use her. The idea of Blaire doing anything with Woods made my skin crawl. I started moving. I didn't stop and think about it, and I didn't give a shit if my sister saw me.

"There is nothing about you that is unwanted. Even Rush isn't that damn blind," Woods was telling her as he moved closer to her. She was trying to get away from him.

"Come here, Blaire," I said, reaching out to take her arm and pull her against me. Woods needed to understand that she was with me. I was protecting her. He should look elsewhere. "I didn't expect you to come tonight," I said in her ear. If I had known she was going to walk out of that room looking like something good enough to eat, I would have guarded the damn door.

"I'm sorry. I thought you said I could come," she whispered, her face turning bright red. I hadn't meant to embarrass her. She misunderstood me.

"I hadn't expected you to show up dressed like that," I explained, keeping my eyes locked on Woods. I didn't want to do this in front of her, but if he pushed me, I would. The little red dress clung to Blaire in ways that should be fucking illegal. Didn't she have a mirror in that room? Hell, I couldn't remember.

Blaire suddenly jerked her arm free of me and started moving toward the kitchen.

"What is your fucking problem, man?" Woods asked, glaring at me and making a move to go after her.

"She's off-limits," I warned him, stepping in front of him to block his path. "You need to stay the hell away from her."

Woods's angry glare heated as he stared at me. "You deciding to claim her now? Making family work at the club is low, even for you, Rush."

I took a step toward him. "Stay out of this, and stay away

from her. That's your only warning," I told him, before walking away to find Blaire.

Grant met me in the hallway. "She's hurt. Go fix it," he said, shooting me an annoyed look as he walked past me and back to the party.

Why was she hurt? What had I done other than keep Woods from using her? I ignored two people and shook my head at Nan as she made her way toward me. I wasn't dealing with her right now.

"Are you going in there?" she hissed angrily at me.

"Go enjoy your very expensive party, little sister." I opened the pantry door and closed it behind me, locking it. I didn't want someone following me inside.

I didn't knock on her door. I knew she wouldn't open it. I opened it instead and stared at her as she stood there, trying to unzip her dress. She let her hands fall back to her sides as she stared at me, then took a step back, bumping into the bed and sitting down. There wasn't much room to move in here, which made me angry. How was she living in this tiny space? I stepped inside and closed the door behind me.

"How do you know Woods?" I asked. The anger in my voice hadn't been intentional.

"His dad owns the country club. He golfs. I serve him drinks," she said nervously.

I knew all that already. I just wanted to make sure that was the only way she knew him. I couldn't stand the idea of her spending time with him. With anyone. "Why did you wear that?" I asked, looking down at the dress that was going to star in my late-night fantasies of her.

Blaire shot back up, and her eyes turned from nervous to heated fast. "Because my mother bought it for me to wear. I was stood up and never got the chance. Tonight you invited me, and I wanted to fit in. So I wore the nicest thing I had. I'm sorry that it wasn't quite nice enough. You know what, though? I don't give a shit. You and your uppity, spoiled friends all need to get over yourselves." Then she shoved me with her hand as if she wanted to knock me over. I didn't move, but she'd put some force behind it.

She didn't get me at all. She didn't understand, and holy hell, she thought she wasn't good enough. Was she kidding me? She was so damn near perfect it hurt. I closed my eyes tightly, trying not to look at her. I had to get away from her. This room was so small. She smelled so good . . .

"Fuck!" I swore, before burying my hands in her hair and covering her lips with mine. I had to taste her. I couldn't control myself. We were alone and too close, and she smelled like heaven.

I had expected Blaire to fight me, but she melted into me so easily. I took what I could while she was still too shocked to slap me. Her mouth moved under mine, and I licked at the swell of her bottom lip. "I've been wanting to taste this sweet, plump lip since you walked into my living room," I told her before taking more. I slid my tongue between her lips, and she opened for me. Each dark corner was better than warm honey. I could get drunk from her taste.

Her small hands grabbed my shoulders and squeezed. I wanted more. I wanted her. She caught on, and her tongue began to move against mine. Then she bit down on my bottom lip. Holy hell.

I grabbed her waist and put her on the bed behind her before covering her body with mine. More. I needed more. More of Blaire. More of her smell. More of her taste. More of the sounds she made. Just fucking more.

When I settled my obvious arousal between the open V of her legs, she moaned and threw her head back. My pulse sped up, and I felt my control slip even further. More.

"Sweet, too sweet," I whispered against her mouth, and I realized I was almost done. I wouldn't be able to stop. And she was sweet. Too fucking sweet for this. I tore myself away from her and backed up off the bed and stared down at her. The sexy red dress was up around her waist, and the pink satin of her panties was right there. The wetness that had darkened them made my blood roar in my veins. "Mother *fucking* shit." I slammed my hand against the wall to keep from reaching for her. Then I opened the door. I had to breathe air that wasn't filled with Blaire. Her smell was all over me. I had to break free.

She was too much. The word *more* kept pounding in my head, reminding me how willing she had been to let me taste her. To touch her. And mother of God, how wet she'd been. I slammed out of the pantry and headed for the door that led outside. Fresh air. Air with no Blaire. Fuck. I wanted her. More. I wanted so much more.

Chapter Eleven

I hadn't slept. All damn night. I had walked for miles along the dark beach and then went to my bedroom and paced the floor. A cold shower hadn't helped, either. Every time I closed my eyes, I saw those pink panties and heard Blaire's sweet sounds. I had to get her out of my head.

I needed to get laid. I hadn't slept with anyone since the incident with Anya. That wasn't like me. Tonight I had to work this out of my system. Keeping Blaire at a distance was all that would keep her from being hurt. It was only a matter of time before she knew and before she hated me.

I grabbed my phone and scanned the numbers I had saved until I found one that I knew was safe for a one-nighter with no strings. She'd require a dinner and some attention first, but Bailey had been trying to get my attention since she'd come to one of Nan's parties. I'd taken her number and said I'd call sometime.

Once I had set a date for tonight, I got ready for my day with Nan. We were playing a round of golf today, her birthday request. I was hoping we would miss Blaire, but if not, I could handle buying a drink from her. I just wouldn't breathe her in when she was near me. Or look at her. And I would not think about her panties. Fuck. I needed another cold shower.

◇

Nan was standing with her arms crossed over her chest and a pout on her face when I walked up to the clubhouse ten minutes late. "Sorry I'm late," I told her, and bent down to kiss her on the cheek to soften her up a bit.

She shoved at my shoulder. "That's not why I'm upset. I just got here," she said, rolling her eyes at me. "Why did I have to hear from Bailey that you asked her out for tonight and not from you?" she asked me, looking annoyed.

Because tonight was about fucking Blaire out of my head. Nothing more. "Didn't know you cared about who I planned to fuck tonight," I replied with a wink, as I pulled my bag out of my Range Rover and handed it to the caddy, who had rushed over to greet me when I drove up.

"Rush, really?" Nan snapped at me.

"When she gave me her number, she knew what she was doing. But if you want to call her and warn her of my plans, then be my guest. I'd much prefer she canceled on me now so I could find a replacement."

Nan shook her head and let out a sigh. "You are horrible."

"You love me," I told her, then grabbed her hand, tugging her with me toward the golf cart. "I want to drive, and I don't need someone to get my clubs for me. Are you good with just me, or do we need a caddy?" I asked her.

She climbed regally into the passenger seat and shrugged. "As long as you intend to get my clubs and clean them, then I don't mind."

"Diva," I muttered, and handed the caddy a hundred-dollar bill for his time, then climbed in and drove us to the first hole.

"Princess, Rush. I'm a princess," she reminded me.

"No, sis, you aren't. You're a spoiled diva. Marrying a royal would be the only way you could be accused of being a princess," I teased.

Nan slapped at my arm and laughed. This was the sister who was easy to deal with. The one who was my friend, who I could be myself with. The one who didn't demand things of me that I couldn't do. "Bailey is really nice. Her daddy is a heart surgeon, and she's designing her own clothing line. I think you'd like her if you gave her more than one night in your bed."

I parked the cart and got out. "She won't be in my bed. I don't ever take them to my bed. My sofa, maybe, possibly my kitchen table. Hell, I may try out the washing machine tonight. Once I figure out where the hell it is. Have you ever washed anything in my house before?" I was trying to change the subject. I didn't want to hear about Bailey and have any guilt over using her body tonight.

"You are impossible!" Nan walked out to the tee, expecting me to get her club. She had been serious about that. She liked to play, but she had no idea what club to choose for each shot.

"I'm horny, and Bailey has some nice tits," I told her.

Nan frowned at me. "I'm warning her that you're a dog. She needs to know."

I handed Nan her driver and smirked. "She knows, sis. She knows, or she wouldn't have given me her number."

Nan waved her hand at me and took the driver.

I had turned to get my own driver when the golf cart coming our way caught my attention. I noticed Blaire's blond hair. Her eyes were focused on me. Shit. I'd known there was a good chance I would see her, but I had hoped that talking about the sex I intended to have with Bailey tonight would cool me down.

I looked away from her. I wasn't going to let her get to me. I could ignore her. Get a drink and act like she was just an average cart girl.

Bethy, one of the other cart girls, was in the front seat with Blaire. She was staring at Nan as she talked. I cringed, thinking of what Bethy might know that she could tell Blaire. I wasn't sure how close the two were. Surely not very close. Bethy was nothing like Blaire. Innocence had long left Bethy.

"You're kidding me. Woods hired her?" Nan hissed. I glanced over at my sister and saw that she had noticed the drinks cart arriving.

"Don't," I warned her, and walked over to stand close enough to Nan to control her if needed.

"Can I get y'all a drink?" Blaire's sweet voice sent chills all over me.

"At least she knows her place," Nan said. She was being cruel, and I needed to stop her, but that would only make Blaire think I was nice. I wasn't nice. She had to see that.

"I'll take a Corona. Lime, please," I said instead.

Blaire's gaze swung to mine, but I quickly looked away from her. "Get a drink. It's hot," I told Nan.

Nan liked that I was blowing Blaire off like she was someone I didn't know. "Sparkling water. Wipe it off, though, because I hate the way it comes out all wet from the water," Nan instructed.

Bethy moved to get the water before Blaire could. That was interesting. She seemed to be protecting Blaire. "Haven't seen you out here lately, Nan," Bethy said as she wiped off the bottle with a towel.

"Probably because you're too busy in the bushes with God knows who spreading your legs instead of working," Nan said.

I could feel the tension rolling off Blaire as she popped the top off my Corona. Her shoulders were straight, and her back was stiff as a board.

"That's enough, Nan," I told her, hoping to end this so they could leave.

Blaire handed me the bottle, and I couldn't ignore her then. She was focusing on anything other than me at the moment, but for just a second, I wanted her to see me. To look at me. Her eyes lifted and met mine, and it hit me hard.

"Thanks," I said, then slipped a bill into her pocket. It was an excuse to touch her and to hide just how much I was tipping her from Nan.

I stepped away and took my sister's elbow. Time to get her away from them. "Come on and show me how you still can't kick my ass out here," I teased.

She played right into my hands. "You're going down," she said, and walked away from the girls.

I heard Bethy whisper to Blaire, and I glanced back and saw her staring at me. A smile touched my lips. I couldn't keep from smiling when I looked at her. I tore my gaze off her and went back to talking to Nan. She was arguing about the driver I had given her.

I liked a cold drink while I played golf, but for the first time ever, I was hoping the drink cart wouldn't find us again this round.

Chapter Twelve

Bailey was sexy. There was no denying it. She wore her tight, expensive dress well, and the heels she had on did amazing things for her legs. Most of the night, she pressed against me and made promises with her eyes. When she let me slip my hand up her dress right there in the restaurant and play with her, I knew she was more than aware of why I had called her.

Nan had worried me with her talk about Bailey being a good girl and being worth more than a quick fuck. Fact was, she was nice. I liked her well enough. She would be great for some guy who wanted that kind of thing. I didn't. I just wanted to get Blaire Wynn out of my head.

Bailey wrapped her arms around me and started kissing and nibbling my neck as I unlocked the front door. Blaire would be here soon. But I wasn't taking Bailey up to my room. I glanced at the clock, and I knew I had about thirty minutes. I'd start it in here and then take her out to the beach some-where dark and hidden. Blaire wouldn't see us. And I wouldn't be thinking about how close she was.

"In a hurry?" I asked as the door opened.

Bailey smiled up at me and puckered up her lips. "Maybe. I've fantasized about having you inside me, Rush Finlay, for so damn long," she said, reaching back and unzipping her dress and shoving it down. Her double-Ds fell free, and large brown nipples greeted me. "I want that dirty mouth on me," she said, pressing her chest out and holding her heavy breasts in her hands. The long, red, perfectly manicured nails pinched her nipples as she backed into the house. "I've gotten off so many times thinking about you sucking my nipples and sliding inside of me, harder and harder," she said in a husky whisper.

I hadn't been hard, but the suggestive image she was painting was helping to get me very interested. Grabbing her waist, I forced myself to keep my eyes on her. To remember who it was I was with. This was not Blaire. I was with Bailey.

"You want this?" I asked, picking her up so that her nipple was at my mouth and her legs wrapped around my waist. Sticking my tongue out, I flicked her nipple with the tongue ring I'd worn, knowing my mouth would be pleasing a woman tonight.

"Yes, God, yes. Suck it!" she cried out.

I enjoyed the fullness of her breast in my hand as I pulled the hard nipple into my mouth. I opened my eyes frequently to remind myself of who this was. I wasn't going to use someone else like that again. If I was gonna fuck her, then I was gonna fuck her. Just her.

She began rubbing herself on my chest. This one was hot. She was gonna blow fast and several times. Good. I needed several times. I threw her onto the sofa, shoved her dress up around her waist, and buried my face back into her cleavage as she cried out my name.

She didn't smell sweet like Blaire. Her sounds weren't soft and sexy. Fuck!

I had to stop this. I shoved her legs apart and slid my

hands into her panties. Glancing down at them, I saw they were black. Not pink. They were also lace, not satin. Nothing like Blaire. This wasn't Blaire.

I slid my fingers inside her, and the wetness pulled me in further. She was ready. More than ready. I was going to exhaust us both.

"Yes, Rush, baby, just like that. Harder. Suck it harder!" she cried out.

I needed her to shut up. This wasn't helping me, dammit.

"Mmm, yes, please touch me," she begged.

"Shhh," I told her, not going near her mouth. I had a thing about mouths. I didn't trust where they had been. I never kissed easily. Her sounds were all wrong. She was too loud. Too . . . too—

A door slammed, and I froze. Shit. I was off Bailey and standing up instantly. "Cover up, pull your dress down," I demanded, and I walked out of the room to stop Blaire before she saw anything. I stuck my hand into my pocket when I thought of Bailey's smell on my fingers.

"She ran out. Whoever it was," Bailey said from behind me, and I stopped walking.

No. Fuck, no. Not this time. Not now. *Hell!*

"Who was that?" Bailey asked behind me.

"Get dressed, I'll take you home," I told her, and headed for the bathroom where I could wash my hands. Blaire had run out. Why did she run? The last time, she'd gone to her room. This time, she ran out and slammed the door.

It was the kiss. I didn't kiss. I fucked. But I'd kissed Blaire. I knew her mouth was clean and sweet. I had wanted it. More.

Always more with her. I always wanted more.

I couldn't have more.

When I stepped out of the bathroom, I headed for the door. I jerked it open, and my heart sank when I noticed that Blaire's truck was gone. She had been here and left. She'd worked in the sun all day. She had to be exhausted and hungry. She needed to come home and get something to eat. She probably wanted a shower. But she was off doing what? Riding around? She didn't even have a damn cell phone. Fuck that. I was getting her a phone. She needed a damn phone.

"Why was she here? Did you double-book?" Bailey asked in a sharp tone. I'd upset her. But I couldn't keep touching her while thinking about Blaire seeing us. I hated the idea of Blaire seeing us.

"No. Let's go," I said. I didn't owe her an explanation about Blaire.

"I don't care. I know this is a one-night thing. I'm aware of how Rush Finlay works. I want that one night, Rush," Bailey said, walking up to me and pulling on my shirt. "I need to be fucked hard. Wherever and however you want it."

Great. Now I had her worked up, and it was going to be even harder to get rid of her. "Listen, that girl . . ." I paused. What was I gonna say? I was using Bailey to get *that girl* out of my head. Now all I could do was think about her. "She—she's special. I need to check on her and get her back here. She's staying here, and what she saw . . . she didn't deserve to see that."

Bailey took a step back. Her heels clicked against the marble floor. "Are you in a relationship?" she asked, incredulously.

I shook my head. "No. I'm not in anything with anyone. But she's . . ." I stopped. Fuck this. I didn't have time for this. "I need to take you home now and find her, or I need to call someone to come get you. I don't have time for this."

Bailey spun on her heels and headed for the door. "Fine, Finlay. But don't ever call me again. This was it. Your one chance. It's over."

Best news I'd heard all damn day.

I took Bailey home and then drove through town, with no sign of Blaire. I hurried back to the house, hoping she'd be there. It was almost midnight, and I was about ready to call the fucking police. She could be hurt somewhere, or someone could have her, or . . . no. I was letting my imagination get ahead of me. She was upset. I had upset her. My stomach knotted up. She had to understand that we couldn't do this. That kiss was it. No more. I wasn't ever going to let there be more for us.

Her truck was still gone when I parked in the garage and headed inside. I would wait for her for fifteen minutes, but then I was calling for backup. I would have a search party looking for her within ten minutes of my call. It was too dangerous for her to run off late like this. Even in Rosemary Beach.

Headlights filled the driveway, and I let out the breath I was holding. She was home. I waited until she was out of the truck and at the door before I opened it. I wasn't giving her a chance to run from me.

She stood there in front of me then glanced around at my feet as if she were expecting to find something.

"Where have you been?" I asked, trying not to sound as frustrated as I was.

"What does it matter?" she asked. She wasn't angry. She looked confused.

I closed the little bit of space between us. "Because I was worried," I said honestly. She needed to know. She'd scared me.

"I find that real hard to believe. You were too busy with your company for the night to notice much of anything." The distaste in her voice was obvious.

"You came in earlier than I expected. I didn't mean for you to witness that," I said, knowing it sounded bad as I said it. But I didn't have an excuse. Even if I wished I did.

She shifted her feet and let out a sigh. "I came home the same time I do every night. I think you wanted me to see you. Why, I'm not sure. I'm not harboring feelings for you, Rush. I just need a place to stay for a few more days. I'll be moving out of your house and your life real soon."

Damn her. She was going to make me feel. I couldn't fucking feel. Not with her. Closing my eyes, I muttered a curse and tried to calm myself down. "There are things about me you don't know. I'm not one of those guys you can wrap around your finger. I have baggage. Lots of it. Too much for someone like you. I expected someone so different, considering I've met your father. But you're nothing like him. You're everything a guy like me should stay away from. Because I'm not right for you."

She laughed. She fucking laughed. I was being honest with her, and she was laughing at me. "Really? That's the best you've got? I never asked you for anything more than a room. I don't expect you to want me. I never did. I am aware that you and

I are on two different playing fields. Your league is one I will never measure up to. I don't have the right bloodlines. I wear cheap red dresses, and I have a fond connection to a pair of silver heels because my mother wore them on her wedding day. I don't need designer things. And *you* are designer, Rush."

That was it. She had pushed me too damn far. I grabbed her hand and pulled her inside my house and backed her up against the wall. Caging her body in with mine felt good. It made my body hum with excitement that it didn't need to be feeling. "I'm not designer. Get that through your head. I can't touch you. I want to so damn bad it hurts like a motherfucker, but I can't. I won't mess you up. You're . . . you're perfect and untouched. And in the end, you would never forgive me." There, let her laugh at me now. The soft O of her lips only had me craving her taste again.

"What if I want you to touch me? Maybe I'm not so untouched. Maybe I'm already tainted."

I wanted to laugh this time. Did she not know that I was aware of what kind of girl she was? I caressed her face, needing to touch her somewhere. "I've been with a lot of girls, Blaire. Trust me, I've never met one as fucking perfect as you. The innocence in your eyes screams at me. I want to peel every inch of your clothing off and bury myself inside you, but I can't. You saw me tonight. I'm a screwed-up, sick bastard. I can't touch you."

"OK," she said, looking almost relieved. Had she been frightened that I wanted more with her? "Can we at least be friends? I don't want you to hate me. I'd like to be friends," she said, looking hopeful.

Friends? She thought I could be her friend? I closed my

eyes so I couldn't see her face. So I couldn't get lost in her eyes. Being her friend wasn't something I was sure I could do, but I knew I couldn't tell this girl no. She was under my skin, and I was done for. I opened my eyes and looked at her heartbreaking, beautiful face. "I'll be your friend. I'll try my damnedest to be your friend, but I have to be careful. I can't get too close. You make me want things I can't have. That sweet little body of yours feels too incredible tucked underneath me," I said, before lowering my head until my lips brushed against her ear. "And the way you taste. It's addictive. I dream about it. I fantasize about it. I know you'll be just as delicious in . . . other places."

She leaned into me, and her breathing hitched. How was I supposed to be friends with her? She was so tempting.

"We can't. Fuck me. We can't. Friends, sweet Blaire. Just friends," I whispered, then moved away from her and headed for the stairs. Space. We needed space. I was going to touch her if I didn't get more space.

I reached the stairs, and the idea of her sleeping underneath them sliced through me. It was bothering me more and more every damn day. But how would I move her closer to me? We needed the space. She was safe under there.

"I don't want you under those damn stairs. I hate it. But I can't move you up here. I'll never be able to stay away from you. I need you safely tucked away," I explained, without looking back at her. I wanted to see if she believed me. I wanted to see her one last time. I wanted . . . more.

I couldn't. I ran the rest of the way up the stairs and to my room, slamming and locking myself inside. I had to stay away from her.

Chapter Thirteen

Grant was meeting me at the gym early this morning. We hadn't gotten into a routine for our workouts yet this summer, but since I wasn't sleeping that great, with Blaire haunting my thoughts, I figured I could get to the gym early with Grant before he went to work.

Blaire was still in her room when I pulled out of the driveway that morning, but the sun wasn't up yet, either. I had to work out some of this aggression. If sex wasn't going to happen anytime soon, then I would beat my body into submission with the weights. Maybe I could sleep after this.

Grant was waiting for me outside the gym in town. It wasn't the one at the club, because Grant said that gym was for pussies. Real men worked out at real gyms, according to him. "About time you got here," he grumbled when I walked up to him.

"Shut up. The sun's not even up yet," I replied.

Grant just grinned and took a swig of his bottled water. "You hydrate this morning?" he asked.

"No. I need some coffee. They have that in this place?"

Grant laughed loudly. "It's a gym, Rush. Not Starbucks. Here," he said, tossing me a bottle of water from his bag. "You need water right now. Coffee later."

"I'm not liking your choice of gyms," I informed him.

"Stop being a girl."

We worked out for more than two hours before I was allowed some coffee. My lesson had been learned for the future: drink a cup before I leave the house.

"Party tonight?" Grant asked as we stepped outside the gym.

"Where?"

"Your place. Just a few people. You need the distraction from your roommate, and I need an excuse to persuade that friend of Nan's—Bailey, I think—to visit my bed," he said.

I winced. "A party at my place isn't the way to make that happen. I had Bailey over last night. Didn't end well."

Grant stopped walking. "What? You didn't get any? She seemed like a damn sure thing to me. I was sure she'd be all over you."

"Blaire saw us before it got too heated, and it got screwed up. I sent Bailey home."

Grant let out a low whistle. "Wow . . . so Blaire caught you, and you sent a girl away," he said, shaking his head. "Dude. We need a party. We need girls over. Not Bailey, since you already went there, but some new girls. Nan has friends. You need to get your head out of Blaire Wonderland. Can't happen. You know that."

I nodded. He was right. It couldn't happen. "Sure. Whatever. Invite who you want."

The crowd was small. I was impressed with Grant for keeping it intimate. I kept my eyes toward the door, waiting for

Blaire to get home. She wasn't prepared for guests. She had to be tired after the late night last night. I intended to keep the music down and to keep people off the stairs so she could sleep. I considered letting her sleep in one of the guest bedrooms just for tonight so she could rest. People could be here late. It could get louder.

No. *No*. I wouldn't be able to stay away from her. Not a good idea. She had to stay under the stairs. It was safer there. She could sleep; I'd make sure she could.

"Rush!" Grant called from the balcony. I glanced back at the door before heading outside to see what he wanted. I couldn't stay out there long. I had to get back to watching for Blaire.

"Yeah?" I asked Grant, who was sitting on the lounge chair with a new girl in his lap. He pointed with his beer bottle toward Malcolm Henry. I hadn't seen him since he had arrived in Rosemary Beach. His parents lived in Seattle, and the last I heard, he was attending Princeton.

"Malcolm can't get tickets to Slacker Demon's Seattle stop next month," Grant said, grinning.

I didn't normally get people tickets to see my dad's band on tour, but Malcolm had been a friend of Grant's growing up. He'd also been close to Tripp Montgomery, and Tripp was my friend. Even if I hadn't seen him since he'd run off a couple of years ago.

"I'll make a call," I told him, and Grant's grin grew.

"Tell anyone, and I'll beat your ass," Grant warned Malcolm, still grinning. "He doesn't dish out tickets for just anyone. He's doing this for me, so don't fuck it up."

Grant had already had one too many tonight. He got very giving and jolly when he was drunk. Which meant he drew me into his charity. I shook my head and walked back inside.

Someone called out, "Hey, Woods," and I stopped walking and jerked around. What the hell was Kerrington doing here? I hadn't invited him, and Grant would have said something if he'd invited him. He knew I wasn't happy with Woods right now.

I stalked to the window and glanced outside to see Blaire's truck parked toward the back of the drive. That annoyed me. They shouldn't have blocked her out. I should have thought about that.

But she was here. And so was Woods. Fuck.

I ignored people and moved past Woods to go directly to the pantry. Blaire was in there. Was she changing? Had she invited Woods over? What the hell was I going to do if she had? We were . . . friends now. Shit. Fuck friends. That didn't even sound possible.

Stopping in the pantry, I watched as she stepped out of her room as if she were leaving. Maybe she was going to see Woods.

"Rush? What's wrong?" she asked, looking sincere.

I waited a moment to respond. I didn't want to scare her or sound harsh. "Woods is here," I finally said, as calmly as I could manage.

"Last time I checked, he was a friend of yours," she said.

Last time I checked, he was hot on her trail. "No. He isn't here for me. He came for someone else," I said.

Blaire's confused expression became annoyed and she crossed her arms under her breasts, which she really didn't need to do if she wanted me to keep my eyes off them. "Maybe he is. Do you have a problem with your friends being interested in me?"

"He isn't good enough. He's a sorry-ass fucker. He shouldn't get to touch you," I replied without thinking. The idea of him doing anything with her made my blood boil.

Blaire seemed to be considering what I had just said. Damn, she was adorable when she was frustrated. "I'm not interested in Woods that way. He is my boss and possibly a friend. That's all."

I wasn't sure what to say to that. I couldn't order her to stay under the damn stairs.

"I can't sleep while people are going up and down the stairs. It keeps me up. Instead of sitting in my room alone, wondering who you're upstairs screwing tonight, I thought I'd talk to Woods out on the beach. Have a conversation with someone. I need friends."

Motherfucker. "I don't want you outside with Woods talking," I said. I wanted to tell her there was no chance I was taking anyone upstairs and fucking them. She had somehow ruined me, and all I'd done was kiss her.

"Well, maybe I don't want you screwing some girl, but you will," she shot back at me. The fierce look on her face made me want to laugh and kiss her senseless at the same damn time.

She was pushing me. I was too close to forgetting why this was a bad idea. I moved toward her, and she backed up until we were back inside her little room. Safe from Woods Kerrington. I wanted to keep her here. "I don't want to fuck anyone tonight," I told her. Then I couldn't keep the amusement off my face. Because that was a lie. "That isn't exactly true. Let me clarify. I don't want to fuck anyone outside of this room. Stay here and talk to me. I'll talk. I said we could be friends. You don't need Woods as a friend."

She shoved me back without much force. "You never talk to me. I ask the wrong question, and you stalk away."

But she had said we were friends. I would play that card all damn night if I had to. "Not now. We're friends. I'll talk, and I won't leave. Just, please, stay in here with me."

She glanced around and frowned. "There isn't a lot of room in here," she said, her hands still flat on my chest. I wondered if she could feel my heart beating. It was hammering so hard I could hear it pounding in my ears.

"We can sit on the bed. We won't touch. Just talk. Like friends," I told her. Anything to get her to stay in here away from Woods.

She relaxed and sat down on the bed, her hands leaving me. I wanted to reach out and grab them and hold them against me. "Then we'll talk," she said, as she scooted back on the bed and crossed her legs.

I sat on the bed and leaned against the other wall. We weren't far apart, but it was as much as this room would allow. The situation made me laugh. "I can't believe I just begged a female to sit and talk to me."

"What are we going to talk about?" she asked, studying me. I could tell by her expression that she expected me to bolt at any moment.

"How about how the hell you're still a virgin at nineteen?" I said, before I could stop myself. She was just too damn beautiful to be that innocent. It made no sense to me.

She stiffened. "Who said I'm a virgin?" she asked, sounding upset.

I'd known she was a virgin from the first time I had caught her checking me out. The blush on her face had been all I needed to know. The girl was innocent. "I know a virgin when I kiss one," I told her instead.

She relaxed again, then shrugged as if it wasn't a big deal. When it was a fucking huge deal. I didn't know nineteen-year-old virgins who looked like her. "I was in love. His name is Cain. He was my first boyfriend, my first kiss, my first make-out session, however tame it may have been. He said he loved me and claimed I was the only one for him. Then my mom got sick. I no longer had time to go on dates and see Cain on the weekends. He needed out. He needed freedom to get that kind of relationship from someone else. So I let him go. After Cain, I didn't have time to date anyone else."

What the hell? She loved this dick, and he left her? "He didn't stick by you when your mom was sick?"

She tensed up again and fiddled with her hands in her lap. "We were young. He didn't love me. He just thought he did. Simple as that." She was defending him. Fuck that. He needed an ass-kicking.

"You're still young," I told her, but I was trying to remind myself more than anything.

"I'm nineteen, Rush. I've taken care of my mother for three years and buried her without any help from my father. Trust me, I feel forty most days," she said. The weariness in her voice hurt my chest. I was wanting to beat some unknown kid's ass when this shit was my fault. My gut twisted and reminded me of how I had played a part in her pain.

I reached for her hand, because I needed to touch her somehow. "You shouldn't have had to do that alone."

She didn't say anything at first. The frown line in her fore-head eased before she lifted her gaze from my hand on hers to my face. "Do you have a job?" she asked.

I laughed. She was changing the subject and directing the

questions at me. Smart move. I squeezed her hand. "Do you believe everyone must have a job once they're out of college?" I asked, teasing her.

She shrugged in response. I could tell that yes, she did think that. My life was something she wasn't used to.

"When I graduated from college, I had enough money in the bank to live the rest of my life without a job, thanks to my dad. After a few weeks of doing nothing but partying, I realized I needed a life. So I began playing around with the stock market. Turns out I'm pretty damn good at it. Numbers were always my thing. I also donate financial support to Habitat for Humanity. A couple of months out of the year, I'm more hands-on, and I work on-site. Summers I take off from everything that I can and come here and relax."

I hadn't meant to tell her the truth—or at least all of it—but I did. It just came out of my mouth. She put me at ease. Women never put me at ease. I was always on guard for their ulterior motive. Blaire didn't have one.

"The surprise on your face is a little insulting," I told her. I was teasing, but it was also the truth. I didn't like her thinking I was a spoiled brat, even though I'd been pushing that idea on her the whole time she'd been living under my roof.

"I just didn't expect that answer," she finally replied.

I needed distance. I could smell her again, and holy hell, she smelled good. I moved back to my side of the bed. Touching time was up.

"How old are you?" she asked.

I was surprised she didn't already know. All she had to do was Google me. "Too old to be in this room with you and way too damn old for the thoughts I have about you," I replied.

"I will remind you that I am nineteen. I'll be twenty in six months. I'm not a baby," she said. She didn't appear nervous at all that I had just admitted to fantasizing about her.

"No, sweet Blaire, you are definitely not a baby. I'm twenty-four and jaded. My life hasn't been normal, and because of it, I have some serious screwed-up shit. I've told you there are things you don't know. Allowing myself to touch you would be wrong." I needed her to understand that. One of us had to remember why I needed to keep my hands off her.

"I think you underestimate yourself. What I see in you is special." Her words made the ache in my chest catch on fire. She didn't know me. Not really. But damn, it felt good to hear her say she saw something other than the rock star's son.

"You don't see the real me. You don't know what all I've done." Because when she did know, moments like this would just be bittersweet memories that haunted me the rest of my life.

"Maybe," she said, and leaned toward me. "But what little I have seen isn't all bad. I'm beginning to think there might just be another layer to you."

Holy hell, she needed to move back. That smell and those eyes. I started to say something but stopped myself. I wasn't sure what to say to her. Other than that I wanted to strip her naked and make her scream my name over and over again.

Something she saw made her eyes go wide, and she moved even closer to me. "What is in your mouth?" she asked, with a touch of amazement in her voice.

I was wearing a barbell in my tongue tonight. I didn't always wear something that could be seen, because I had outgrown the piercing, or at least I felt like that at times. Females, however, enjoyed it. I opened my mouth and stuck out my tongue so Little Miss Curious could see. She had already angled her head to peek inside my mouth. If I didn't show her, she was going to climb into my lap to get closer.

"Does it hurt?" she asked in a whisper, still inching closer to me. What the hell? She was gonna get a real personal view of it when I licked her damn neck if she didn't back up.

"No," I replied, keeping my tongue in my mouth for fear that she was going to actually touch it and make me lose my mind.

"What are the tattoos on your back?" she asked me, moving back some. Her smell still clung to me. I was inhaling more frequently than necessary just to get her scent inside of me. It was pathetic. *Focus on something else. Answer her damn questions, and stop thinking about her skin. And her taste. Tattoos . . . she wants to know about my tattoos.*

"An eagle on my lower back with his wings spread and the emblem for Slacker Demon. When I was seventeen, my dad took me to a concert in L.A., and afterward he took me to get my first tat. He wanted his band branded on my body. Every member of Slacker Demon has one in the exact same place. Right behind the left shoulder. Dad was high as a kite that night, but it is still a really good memory. I didn't get a chance to spend a lot of time with him growing up. But every time I saw him, he added another tat or piercing to my body," I explained.

Her eyes instantly went to my chest. Fuck, she was wondering about my nipples. Cold shower. I was going to need a very long cold shower. Or maybe hot, with some damn baby oil and my fist. God knows her smell and the view I had down her shirt were enough to send me over the edge.

"No piercings there, sweet Blaire. The others are in my ears. I put a halt to the piercings and tats when I turned nineteen," I assured her. She needed to take her eyes off my damn chest. Now.

She looked unhappy or worried. What had I said? Fuck, I hadn't verbalized my shower plans, had I?

"What did I say to make you frown?" I asked, touching her chin to tilt her eyes up so I could see them.

"When you kissed me last night, I didn't feel the silver barbell thingy." That was what was making her frown? She was going to kill me. I couldn't take much more of this.

"Because I wasn't wearing it," I said, moving closer to her. Her scent was pulling me in.

"When you, uh, kiss someone with it in, can she feel it?"

Holy fucking hell. Showing Little Miss Curious was so tempting. She wanted to experience it, and I sure wanted to show her. "Blaire, tell me to leave. Please," I begged. It was the only way to keep from kissing her. "You would feel it. Everywhere I want to kiss you, you would feel it. And you would enjoy it," I whispered in her ear, then pressed a kiss to her shoulder and inhaled her deeply. Fuck, that was good.

"Are you . . . are you going to kiss me again?" she asked, as I ran my nose up her neck, soaking in her scent. Damn smell was intoxicating.

"I want to. I want to so fucking bad, but I'm trying to be good," I admitted.

"Could you not be good for just one kiss? Please?" she

asked, moving closer to me. Her legs pressed up against mine. One more inch, and she'd be in my lap.

"Sweet Blaire, so incredibly sweet." I was losing it. My lips were touching every smooth inch of skin they could as I fought with myself not to touch her. She was innocent. She was too good for me. This was wrong.

I tasted her skin with the tip of my tongue, and my cock throbbed. She was delicious. Everything about her. I kissed a trail up her neck, and when I reached her lips, I stopped. I wanted them. I wanted her. More. Always more. But she was my . . . friend. I had caused her pain, and she didn't even know it. I had to stop this.

"Blaire, I'm not a romantic guy. I don't kiss and cuddle. It's all about the sex for me. You deserve someone who kisses and cuddles. Not me. I just fuck, baby. You aren't meant for someone like me. I've never denied myself something I want. But you're too sweet. This time, I have to tell myself no," I said, more to myself than to her. I needed to remind myself just how out of my league she was.

She whimpered, and I jumped up, moving to the door. I wouldn't do this to her. I couldn't.

"I can't talk anymore. Not tonight. Not alone in here with you," I said, and left before I lost myself with her. I could never have Blaire.

Chapter Fourteen

I stalked past the few people in the kitchen and headed for the front door. I needed to go outside and calm down. Fresh air with no one around to see me lose my shit. Telling Blaire no had just about killed me. Turning down those sweet, willing lips . . . Holy hell, no man should be put through this torture.

"Want to talk about it?" Grant asked, as the door behind me closed.

"I need to be alone," I told him. I gripped the porch railing and kept my eyes focused on the driveway full of cars.

"You aren't gonna be able to keep this up. She's under your skin now," Grant said, coming to stand beside me. I should have known he'd ignore my request for him to leave me to my thoughts.

"I won't hurt her," I told him.

Grant sighed and turned to lean against the railing and face me while crossing his hands over his chest. "As sweet as Blaire is, I'm not worried about her. I'm more worried about you," he said.

"I got this."

"No. You don't. You're keeping your hands off her when it's obvious to anyone who sees her look at you that she would let you touch her any way you wanted to. But you're not touching her. I've never—and I mean fucking never—seen you turn that down from someone who looks like Blaire. Which means . . . you've got feelings for her. That's why I'm worried about you. She's gonna find out about her dad and about Nan, and when she does, she'll run like hell. She'll hate all of you. I don't want to see you hurt."

"I know," I said. I fucking knew that. It was why I wasn't hauling her up to my room and locking her there with me. I couldn't go there with her.

"She's outside in the back with Woods," Grant said.

Standing up straight, I let go of the railing and looked back at the door. "How do you know?"

"Saw her walk out there before I came after you," he replied.

I wasn't letting Woods near her, either. He would hurt her. He'd use her, and no one was going to use Blaire. No one. Ever. I would fucking make sure of it. "I gotta go get her. I upset her," I said, heading for the door.

"He knows she's innocent. Woods isn't an asshole. He's a good guy. Stop acting like he's a fucking horndog."

I tightened my grip on the door handle and took a deep breath. "Don't tell me what to do, Grant."

He let out a short laugh. "Never, brother. Never."

I jerked the door open and stepped back inside, intent on finding Blaire and sending Woods home.

"Heeey, Ruuush!" a female slurred excitedly, and she latched on to my arm. I glanced down to see one of Nan's friends whose name I couldn't remember holding on to me.

"No," I replied, and I kept walking. She didn't let go. Instead, she kept giggling and talking about her wet panties. This shit used to turn me on, but the smell of Blaire and the thought of her big eyes as she crawled closer to me so she could study my tongue made everything else seem cheap.

"I'm Babs. Remember? I used to stay the night with your sister in high school," she said, pressing against me.

"Not interested," I told her, trying to jerk free when we stepped into the kitchen and my eyes locked on Blaire. She was alone. No Woods. And she was watching me. With . . . Babs, or whoever this was on my arm. Shit.

"But you said," Babs started to argue. I had no idea what she thought I said. Then she kissed my arm. Fuck. "I'll take off my panties down here if you will," the girl continued, not taking no for an answer. She was wobbling on her heels and clinging to me even more now.

"Babs, I've already told you no. I'm not interested," I repeated loudly, keeping my eyes locked on Blaire's. I wanted her to hear me. I knew this wasn't what I wanted. Who I wanted.

"It'll be naughty," she promised me, then started laughing. Nothing about her was appealing.

"No, it will be annoying. You're drunk, and your cackling is giving me a headache," I said, still looking at Blaire. She had to believe me.

Blaire dropped her eyes from mine and turned to go to the pantry. Good. She was safe in there, and she needed sleep.

"Hey, that girl is going to steal your food," Babs whispered loudly.

Blaire's face turned bright red, and I threw Babs off my arm, letting her stumble to catch herself. "She lives here; she can have whatever she wants," I informed anyone else who might say something to embarrass her.

Blaire's eyes swung back to meet mine again.

"She lives here?" Babs asked.

The hurt in Blaire's eyes burned a hole in my chest. I couldn't take it.

"Don't let him lie to you," Blaire said. "I'm the unwelcome guest living under his stairs. I've wanted a few things, and he keeps telling me no."

Fuck.

She slammed the door behind her. I wanted to go after her, but I knew if I went in there, I wasn't coming out. I wouldn't be able to keep my hands and mouth off her.

Woods walked into the kitchen and swung his gaze to me. "You don't deserve her," he said coldly.

"Neither do you," I replied, then turned and headed for the stairs. I had to get away from these people.

Grant met me in the hallway.

"Make sure Woods leaves. If Blaire comes out of her room, come get me," I said, without stopping to look at him. Then I headed for my room. So I could remind myself, yet again, why I couldn't touch Blaire.

Could you not be good for just one kiss? Please? Those words had kept me up all damn night. How the hell I'd walked out of that little room I had no idea. I had to stop this. I couldn't let her in anymore. She didn't know the truth. I had to protect her. My feelings for her were already too dangerous.

As much as I wanted to tell her about Nan, I couldn't. She'd hate me, and I was too far gone now. I couldn't live with Blaire hating me. At least not this soon. I wasn't ready for her to leave me. I glanced back over my shoulder at the closed pantry door. Last night, Blaire's parting comments about her being the unwelcome guest had pissed me off. I was changing that. Maybe I wasn't ready to move her upstairs yet, but I would feed her. I wasn't sure what she was eating in the mornings, but since she was sleeping in late today, I had time to make her breakfast.

The pantry door opened behind me, and I glanced back again to see Blaire staring at me with a surprised look on her face. We hadn't ended things well last night. This morning, I was going to change that.

"Good morning. Must be your day off."

She didn't move and gave me a forced smile. "Smells good."

"Get out two plates. I make some killer bacon." I was going to soften her up. I knew she was still mad at me for leaving her last night, but dammit, I had done it for her. Not me.

"I've already eaten, but thank you," she said, then bit down on her lower lip as she looked longingly at the bacon. What the hell was that all about? And when had she eaten? I'd been up for two hours, and she hadn't been out of her room.

I set down the fork I was using and focused on her instead of the bacon. "How have you already eaten? You just woke up." I watched her carefully in case she decided not to tell me the complete truth. If this was about her not wanting to eat in front of me or some ridiculous girl issue like that, she was going to have to get over it.

"I keep peanut butter and bread in my room. I had some before I came out."

What the hell did she just say? "Why do you keep peanut butter and bread in your room?" I asked.

She nibbled nervously on her lip a moment, then let out a sigh. "This isn't my kitchen. I keep all my things in my room."

She kept all her things in her room? Wait . . . what? "Are you telling me that you only eat peanut butter and bread when you're here? That's it? You buy it and keep it in your room, and that is all you eat?" A sick knot had formed in my stomach that I hadn't felt since I was a kid. If she told me all she ate was fucking peanut-butter sandwiches, I was going to lose it. Had I made her think she couldn't eat my food? *Fuck!*

She nodded slowly. Those big eyes of hers were even bigger now. I was an asshole. No . . . I was worse than an asshole.

I slammed my hand against the counter and focused on the bacon while I tried like hell to get control of myself.

This was my fault. Fuck me, this was all my fault. She never complained when any other woman on the planet would have. And she was eating motherfucking peanut-butter sandwiches every day. My chest hurt. I couldn't do this anymore. I'd tried. I was done keeping her at a distance.

"Go get your stuff and move upstairs. Take any room on the left side of the hall you want. Throw that damn peanut butter away, and eat whatever the hell you want in this kitchen," I told her.

She remained frozen in her spot. Why wasn't she listening to me?

"If you want to stay here, Blaire, move your ass upstairs now. Then come down here and eat something out of my *motherfucking* fridge while I watch," I growled. She stiffened at my response. I needed to calm down. I didn't want to scare her; I just wanted her to move upstairs, dammit. And eat some bacon!

"Why do you want me to move upstairs?" she asked softly.

I moved the last piece of bacon to the paper towel before looking at her again. Seeing her hurt me physically. Knowing that I'd treated her so poorly and that she'd taken it was making it hard to fucking breathe. "Because I want you to. I hate going to bed at night and thinking about you asleep under my stairs. Now I have the image of you eating those damn peanut-butter sandwiches all alone in there, and it's a little more than I can deal with." There, I'd said it.

She didn't argue this time. She turned around and walked back into the pantry. I stood there and waited until she walked back out, carrying her suitcase in one hand and a jar of peanut butter and some bread in the other. She put the jar and the bread on the counter without looking at me and walked toward the hallway.

I was working to hold on to the edge of the counter to keep from grabbing the jar of peanut butter and smashing it against the wall. I wanted to hit something. The ache inside was taking over, and I needed to hurt something to ease the anger. Anger that was directed completely at myself for being a self-absorbed ass. I had been so fucking worried about not touching her that I'd neglected her in other ways. She was living off fucking peanut butter.

"I don't have to move upstairs. I like that room." Blaire's soft voice broke into my thoughts, and I had to grip the counter even tighter. I'd mistreated her. Neglected her needs. All I wanted was to touch her and fucking smell her and hold her, but I'd let her down. I wasn't going to be able to forgive myself for this.

"You belong in one of the rooms upstairs. You don't belong

under the stairs. You never did," I said, without looking at her.

"Would you at least tell me which room to take? I don't feel right picking one out. This isn't my house."

I was scaring her. One more thing she didn't deserve. I let go of my grip on the counter and looked over at her. She seemed ready to bolt back to the pantry at any minute.

"The rooms on the left are all guest rooms. There are three of them. I think you'll enjoy the view from the last one. It looks out over the ocean. The middle room is all white with pale pink accents. It reminds me of you. So you go choose. Whichever one you want. Take it, then come down here and eat."

"But I'm not hungry. I just ate—"

"If you tell me you ate that damn peanut butter again, I am going to throw it through a wall." Fuck, the thought of that made me furious. I took a deep breath and focused on sounding calm. "Please, Blaire. Come eat something for me."

She nodded her head and climbed the stairs. I should have taken her suitcase for her, but I knew she didn't want me near her right now. She needed to do this alone. I'd just acted like a crazy man. I washed out the skillet that I'd cooked the bacon in. Once it was put away and Blaire still hadn't come back downstairs from choosing her room, I took a large plate out of the cabinet and filled it with eggs and bacon before sitting down at the table. She could eat off my plate.

Blaire stepped into the kitchen, and I looked up to see her staring at me. "Did you choose a room?" I asked.

She nodded and walked over to stand on the other side of the table. "Yes. I believe so. The one you said had a great view, is it . . . green and blue?"

"Yes, it is." I couldn't keep from smiling. I liked that she'd chosen the one I thought she would. Even if it was the room closest to me.

"And you're OK with me staying in that room? It is really nice. I'd want that room if this were my house." She was still making sure that I wouldn't change my mind and toss her back under the stairs.

I smiled at her reassuringly "You haven't seen my room yet." I had said *yet*. I was going to cave in. I didn't take girls to my room. It was mine. But I wanted to see her there. With my things.

"Is your room on the same floor?" she asked.

"No, mine takes up the entire top floor," I explained.

"You mean all those windows? That's all one big room?" The awe in her voice was hard to miss. I would be taking her up there to see it before it was all over.

"Yep." I ate a piece of bacon while trying to correct my wayward thoughts of Blaire in my room. That would never be a good idea. "Did you already put your things away?" I asked, trying to think about something else. Anything else.

"No, I wanted to check with you before I unpacked. I should probably just keep everything in the suitcase. By the end of next week, I'll be ready to move out. My tips at the club are good, and I've saved almost all of it."

No. She couldn't live alone. That wasn't safe. She thought she had to move because of me. Her sorry-ass father hadn't even called to check on her. She had no one, and she was so damn vulnerable. Someone needed to protect her. She wasn't moving out of this house. I couldn't stand to think of someone hurting her. I kept my focus on the beach outside, hoping it would calm me, but the panic setting in at the thought of her living alone was taking over. "You can stay as long as you want to, Blaire," I assured her. I needed her here.

She didn't respond. I pulled out the chair beside me.

"Sit next to me and eat some of this bacon." She sat down slowly, and I pushed my plate over to her. "Eat," I told her.

She picked up a piece of bacon and took a bite. Her eyes did a fluttery thing that made her lashes fan across her cheekbone. Fuck me, that was sexy as hell.

I nudged the plate toward her again. "Eat another." She was grinning at me like she found this funny, and the ache inside me eased. I could keep her here. I would make it so that she never wanted to leave. "What are your plans for today?" I asked her.

"I don't know yet. I thought I'd look for an apartment, maybe."

There went my ease. Fuck no, she was not looking for an apartment. "Stop talking about moving out, OK? I don't want you moving until our parents get home. You need to talk to your dad before you run off and start living alone. It isn't exactly safe. You're too young."

She laughed. That soft, musical sound that I heard so infrequently. "I am not too young. What is it with you and my age? I am nineteen. I'm a big girl. I can live on my own safely. Besides, I can hit a moving target better than most police officers. My skills with a gun are pretty impressive. Stop with the unsafe-and-too-young thing."

The idea of Blaire and a gun excited and terrified me all at once. As sexy as that sounded, I was also worried about her hurting herself. "So you really do have a gun?"

She grinned and nodded.

"I thought Grant was just being funny. His sense of humor sucks sometimes."

"Nope. I pulled it on him when he surprised me my first night here."

Now, that made me laugh. "I'd love to have seen that."

She just smiled and kept her head down. She wasn't looking at me, and I knew that her first night here wasn't a pleasant memory.

"I don't want you to stay here just because you're young. I get that you can take care of yourself, or you at least think you can. I want you here because . . . I like having you here. Don't leave. Wait until your dad gets back. It sounds like you two are way overdue for a visit. Then you can decide what you want to do. For now, how about you go upstairs and unpack? Think of all the money you can save living here. When you do move out, then you'll have a nice padded bank account." I had just said way more than I wanted to. But I needed to get her to stay.

"OK. If you really mean that, then thank you."

Thoughts of her in my bed naked started taunting me. I couldn't let it turn into that. I had to remember Nan. And what that all meant to Blaire. She'd hate me in the end.

"I mean it. But that also means that the friends thing with us needs to remain in full effect," I told her.

"Agreed," she replied. I hadn't wanted her to agree. I'd wanted her to beg me like she had last night. Because at this moment, I was weak, and I'd give in. I forced all sexual thoughts of Blaire out of my mind. I couldn't think like this, or I would go mad.

"Also, you are going to start eating the food in this house when you're here."

She shook her head at me.

"Blaire, this isn't up for argument. I mean it. Eat my damn food."

She stood up and leveled me with a determined glare. "No. I will buy food and eat it. I am not . . . I'm not like my father."

Fuck. Again, this was all my damn fault. I stood up to look her directly in the eyes. "You think I don't know that by now? You've been sleeping in a damn broom closet without complaint. You clean up after me. You don't eat properly. I am aware that you're nothing like your dad. But you *are* a guest in my home, and I want you eating in my kitchen and treating it like it's yours."

Blaire's stiff shoulders eased a little. "I'll put my food in your kitchen and eat it in here. Will that be better?"

No. That wasn't better. I wanted her eating my food! "If all you intend to buy is peanut butter and bread, then no. I want you eating properly."

She started to shake her head, and I reached out and grabbed her hand.

"Blaire, it will make me happy to know you're eating. Henrietta buys the groceries once a week and stocks this place, expecting me to have a lot of company. There is more than enough. Please. Eat. My. Food."

She bit her bottom lip but not before a giggle escaped. Damn, that was cute.

"Are you laughing at me?" I asked, feeling the need to grin myself.

"Yeah. A little," she replied.

"Does this mean you're gonna eat my food?"

She let out a heavy sigh, but she was still smiling. "Only if you let me pay you weekly."

I shook my head no, and she jerked her hand free and started to walk away. Damn stubborn woman! "Where are you going?" I asked her.

"I'm done arguing with you. I will eat your food if I pay for my part. That's the only deal I will agree to. So take it or leave it."

I growled, but I was going to have to give in. "OK, fine. Pay me."

She glanced back at me. "I'm going to go unpack. Then take a bath in that big ol' tub, and then I don't know. I don't have plans until tonight."

Tonight? "With who?" I asked, not sure I liked the sound of that.

"Bethy."

"Bethy? The cart girl Jace messes around with?" I really didn't like the sound of that. Bethy was nothing but trouble. She'd get drunk and forget all about Blaire. I thought about the men who could hurt her. No, she wasn't going without me. Someone needed to protect her sexy ass.

"Correction. The cart girl Jace *used to* mess around with. She wised up and is moving on. Tonight we're going honky-tonking to pick us up some hardworking blue-collar men." She turned and hurried up the steps.

This conversation wasn't over.

Chapter Fifteen

She was upstairs now. Right next to the door leading up to my room. Taking a bath . . . *Shit*.

I had to leave. Putting space between us today was important. This morning with her had been good. I wasn't going to keep her at a distance so that her basic needs were neglected anymore. She would eat my food, dammit. She would sleep in a good bed and bathe in a nice big bathroom. No more treating her like the fucking help.

The weight off my shoulders was now replaced with fear. Fear that I wouldn't be able to stay away from her. Knowing she was right there, asleep. Watching her eat, which I would now be doing regularly to make sure she ate normal food. I wasn't going to be able to stay away.

Grant. I needed to talk to Grant. He'd remind me of why I couldn't have her. Why I couldn't tuck her into my arms and hold on. After glancing up at the stairs one more time, I headed for the door. Getting some breathing room away from her and talking to someone rational would be good for me.

I climbed inside my Range Rover and dialed my mother's number. They had to be coming home soon. I was running out of time. Blaire would know everything, and I would lose her. I would make sure she was taken care of, though. I wasn't going to just let her run. I'd hold a damn gun on Abe if I had to in order to get him to go after her. Stupid fucker.

"Rush," my mother said after the third ring.

"When are you coming home?" I asked. I wasn't in the mood for small talk.

"I'm not sure. We haven't discussed it," she replied. The annoyed tone in her voice didn't surprise me. She hated knowing that I could make her come home now if I wanted to.

"Let me talk to Abe."

She sighed dramatically. "Why, Rush? So you can yell at him for not being there for his adult daughter who can take care of herself now?"

Gripping the steering wheel, I took several deep breaths and reminded myself that cursing out my mother wasn't cool. This was just her being her self-centered self. "Credit cards, houses, cars—it's all mine, Mom," I reminded her instead.

She made a noise that sounded like a hiss.

"Hello, Rush." Abe's voice came over the phone.

"She has a job at the club. Says she's going to move out and get her own place soon," I told him. Surely he could see how Blaire's living alone was a bad idea.

"Good. I knew she'd be able to figure things out," he said.

I jerked the Range Rover over onto the side of the road. My blood pounded in my ears, and my vision went blurry. Motherfucking piece of shit. Did he really just say that? "You don't deserve to breathe air, you sorry son of a bitch," I growled into the phone.

He didn't reply.

"She's a fucking innocent. She's so damn innocent and trusting. She's gorgeous. Blindingly gorgeous. Head-turning, drop-dead gorgeous. Do you get that? Your daughter has no one. *No one.* And she's vulnerable. She's hurt and alone. Any jackass could use her. Don't you care?" I was breathing hard. My knuckles turned white where I gripped the steering wheel, trying to control my rage.

"She has you," was his only response.

"Me? She has me? What the fuck are you talking about? You know me. I'm Dean Finlay's son. Who am I? I'm sure as hell not her protector. I'm the heartless asshole who took her father away from her when she needed him most. That's who the fuck I am!" Me. He'd said she had me. As if I were worthy of that responsibility. Didn't he cherish her? How could a father have a daughter like Blaire and not want to protect her?

"I would have left without your visit, Rush. I couldn't stay. She hasn't needed me in years. She doesn't need me now. I'm not what she needs. But you . . . maybe you are."

How the fuck did he think that made sense?

"She'll be OK. She'll be much better without me. 'Bye, Rush," Abe said, with a heaviness to his voice that I hadn't heard before. Then the line went dead.

He had hung up.

I sat there staring at the road ahead of me. He wasn't going to do anything for her. He was really going to let her figure things out on her own. And he had a small hope that I'd help her. That was it.

She would be fine. I would make sure of it. She'd be motherfucking perfect. I wouldn't let anyone hurt her. I'd protect her. She didn't have a father to keep her safe, but she had me. She wasn't alone. Not anymore.

She had me.

I didn't want to talk to Grant anymore. I needed to be alone. To think. To plan. Blaire was mine to protect. I had to make sure I didn't let her down again. She deserved so damn much.

◇

I came home hours later with a newfound determination. I would be Blaire's friend. I would be her best friend. Fucking best damn friend she ever had. Nothing would touch her or hurt her. She wouldn't want me making things easy or taking care of her, so I would have to do it quietly. Make her think she was handling it.

I opened the door, a smile touching my lips. Knowing she was inside made things seem right with the world. Until I saw her on the steps dressed like a fucking wet dream.

Holy hell, why was she wearing that?

A short denim skirt with boots—cowboy boots . . . dear Lord, have mercy. "Day-um," I muttered, closing the door behind me. She was going out in that. To the club . . . with Bethy. Shit. "You, uh, wearing that out to go clubbing?" I asked, trying not to let her hear the panic in my voice.

"It's called honky-tonking. I'm pretty sure it's a completely different thing," she said, smiling at me nervously.

A bar. She was going to a bar. Dressed like that.

I ran my hand through my hair and tried to remind myself that she wanted us to be friends. Friends didn't lose their shit and demand that each other change clothes before leaving the house.

"Can I come with y'all tonight? I've never been honky-tonking," I said.

Blaire's eyes went wide. "You want to go with us?"

I let my gaze travel down her body again. Oh hell, yes, I did. "Yeah, I do."

She shrugged. "OK. If you really want to. We need to leave in ten minutes, though. Bethy is expecting me to pick her up."

She was going to let me go. No argument. Thank God. "I can be ready in five," I assured her, and took off up the stairs. I could get changed and down here in plenty of time. Drunk men in a bar with Blaire looking like an angel in a pair of cowboy boots was not happening. At least not without me there to beat them off her.

If I was going to a damn country bar, I was going looking like the son of Dean Finlay. Country bars weren't my thing, although Blaire's boots were definitely on my list of favorite things. Any reason to see her in those boots was a plus.

I grabbed a Slacker Demon shirt and threw it on with my jeans. Then I added my thumb ring. I brushed my teeth and added deodorant before stopping and looking at myself in the mirror. I was missing something.

I grabbed a few of the small hoops I wore on occasion and slid them into my ear. Sticking out my tongue, I grinned, thinking about Blaire's interest in my tongue piercing. She was almost in my lap last night trying to look at it. If she attempted that tonight, I might just let her crawl all over me. Shaking my head at my thoughts, which would lead to nothing but trouble, I ran for the stairs. I hadn't taken ten minutes, but I was pushing it.

On my way back down the stairs, my eyes found Blaire, who was watching me closely. It made my heart speed up when she looked at me like I was some kind of treat. God knows I had thought about tasting her in many, many ways. The idea of her having any naughty thoughts about me got me more excited than I needed to be in these tight jeans.

When her eyes made it to my face, I stuck out my tongue so she could see the piercing. Her eyes flared, and I wanted to groan. Damn, the things I wanted to show her with this little piece of silver.

"I figure if I'm going to a honky-tonk with guys in boots and cowboy hats, I need to stay true to my roots. Rock and roll is in my blood. I can't pretend to fit in anywhere else," I explained.

She laughed. "You're going to look as out of place tonight as I do at your parties. This should be fun. Come on, rock-star spawn," she said, looking pleased before heading toward the door.

I hurried around her and opened the door for her. Something else I should have been doing all along. "Since your friend is riding with us, why don't we take one of my cars? We'd all be more comfortable than in your truck," I suggested. I wanted her sitting up front with me. Close to me. So I could look at those legs . . . and boots. I didn't want to be crammed into a truck with Bethy.

She glanced over her shoulder at me. "But we'd fit in better if we took my truck."

I pulled out the small remote from my pocket to open the door to the garage where my Range Rover was parked. Blaire swung her gaze over and watched as the door opened.

"That's certainly impressive," she said.

"Does that mean we can take mine? I'm not crazy about sharing a seat with Bethy. The girl likes to touch things without permission," I said. She'd never touched me, but I had heard about her.

"Yes, she does. She's a bit of a flirt, isn't she?" Blaire said, grinning.

"'Flirt' is a kind word for her," I replied.

"OK. Sure. We can take the badass Rush Finlay's killer wheels, if he insists," Blaire said with a shrug.

Score. Now I needed to get her into the passenger seat before she tried to climb into the back. I headed toward the Range Rover, nodding for her to follow.

I opened the door for her, and she stopped and looked up at me. "Do you open all your friends' car doors?"

I never opened doors for girls. It made them expect more. But with Blaire, I wanted to. I wanted her to feel cherished. Damn, this was dangerous. "No," I told her honestly, and moved away to get in on my side. I shouldn't flirt. I shouldn't treat her like there could be more.

I climbed in. I wasn't sure what to say to her now.

"I'm sorry. I didn't mean to sound rude," she said, breaking the silence.

I was making this weird for her. I had to work on that if this was going to work. "No. You're right. I just don't have any female friends, so I'm not good at balancing what I should do and what I shouldn't."

"So you open doors for your dates? That's a very chival-rous thing to do. Your mother raised you right." She almost sounded jealous. But . . . no. That made no sense.

"Actually, no, I don't. I . . . you just seem like the kind of girl who deserves to have her door opened. It just made sense in my head at the moment. But I get what you're saying. If we're going to be friends, I need to draw a line and stay behind it."

A small smile touched her lips. "Thank you for opening it for me. It was sweet."

I just shrugged. I wasn't sure I could say more without sounding like an idiot.

"We need to pick Bethy up at the country club. She'll be at the office back behind the clubhouse at the golf course. She had to work today. She's showering and dressing there," Blaire explained.

I pulled out of the driveway and turned toward the club. Blaire and Bethy seemed like two completely different people. The idea of them being friends didn't fit. "How did you and Bethy become friends?"

"We worked together one day. I think we were both in need of a friend. She's fun and free-spirited. Everything I'm not."

I couldn't help but laugh. "You say that like it's a bad thing. You don't want to be like Bethy. Trust me."

She didn't argue with me. At least she knew that Bethy was not someone to imitate. When she didn't say anything else, I focused on getting us to the club and not staring at her legs, which she'd just crossed, making her skirt even shorter. Blaire had great legs. The little bit of sun she'd gotten on the beach made her skin glow.

The idea of those legs wrapped around me made me tremble. I kept my eyes on the road, and when she shifted, I didn't look down. She was moving her legs. Damn.

When I parked in front of the office, she opened the door immediately and jumped down. Shit. Was she moving to let Bethy into the passenger seat? I didn't want Bethy next to me.

Blaire had started for the door when it opened, and out stepped Bethy, dressed like she charged for sex. Red leather shorts? Really?

"What the hell are you doing in one of Rush's rides?" she asked, looking at the Range Rover and then back at Blaire.

"He's going with us. Rush wants to check out a honky-tonk, too. So . . ." Blaire glanced back at me.

"This is seriously going to cramp your chances of picking up a man. Just saying," Bethy said, as she walked down the steps. Then she paused and took in Blaire's outfit. "Or not. You look hot. I mean, I knew you were gorgeous, but you look really hot in that outfit. I want me some real cowgirl boots. Where'd you get those?" No shit. She looked fucking amazing. I hadn't spent time around Bethy, but I liked the fact she wasn't too catty to admit that Blaire looked amazing.

"Thank you, and as for the boots, I got them for Christmas two years ago from my mom. They were hers. I had loved them since she bought them, and after she got, after . . . she got sick, she gave them to me."

My chest constricted. I hadn't known they were her mother's. Fuck. I'd been thinking about doing naughty things to her in them, and they were a memory from her mother. I felt like an ass.

"Your mom got sick?" Bethy asked. Apparently, they hadn't talked much. Or was I the only one Blaire had told about her mom?

"Yeah. But that's another story. Come on, let's go find us some cowboys," Blaire said, waving off her question. She wanted to find a cowboy. Damn, that made it hard to breathe. She wouldn't have a hard time finding a man with a pulse.

They were all going to come running when they saw her. I couldn't hinder her fun time. She'd never let me come with her again.

Finding a way to stay close and watch her without getting in the way was going to be tricky. And hard as fuck. I was going to want to rip the arms off anyone who touched her. I wasn't making any promises if someone touched her ass. It would be on then.

Bethy sauntered toward the Range Rover, grinning at me like she knew my secret. Then she walked past the passenger door and opened the door to the backseat. "I'll let you ride up front, because I have a sneaky feeling that is where the driver wants you," she said, as she let her hair fall over her face and winked at me.

Huh. This girl wasn't so bad after all.

Blaire climbed back into the front seat and smiled at me. "Time to get our country on," she said with a twinkle in her eye.

Chapter Sixteen

Rush Finlay going to the honky-tonk. My, my, my, what a funny thought," Bethy said in an amused tone that said she understood exactly why I was here.

"Funny," I agreed. "Where we headed, Bethy?" I asked her, to distract her from going any further with the teasing and embarrassing Blaire.

"Head toward the Alabama line. It's about thirty miles that way," she told me. I'd figured it had to be a drive. No places in Rosemary Beach or its surrounding areas were where you would find honky-tonk patrons.

Bethy talked about work that day and all that Blaire had missed. Some drama with cart girls. Apparently, one had the hots for Jimmy, who was a server in the restaurant at the club. She got mad at another girl because she was flirting with Jimmy. Jimmy was well loved among the cougars at the club, too. Problem was, Jimmy preferred men. It was a big secret, because Jimmy liked the tips he got from the older female members. So they were all wasting their time. Most people didn't know he batted for the other team.

Blaire found this funny, and I enjoyed listening to her laugh. I even turned the music down so I could focus on what she was saying to Bethy. She tried to include me some, but mostly she listened to Bethy talk.

We pulled up in front of a bar I recognized. I should have known we were headed here when Bethy had said to head toward the Alabama state line. This wasn't just any bar. It was a famous one. Rednecks from all over made their way here to have a beer.

Blaire opened her own door before I could get to her. I decided to back off some and let her enjoy herself. At least the best that I could. I walked beside them as Bethy explained about the bar and why it was famous. After opening the door to the bar, I stepped back and let the girls enter. Blaire's eyes were wide as she took in the place. Bethy explained that the live band would start up soon, and Blaire's smile got bigger. I didn't look around. I knew men were checking her out, and I wasn't sure I could handle it. I kept my focus on her. Then Bethy mentioned tequila shots. Bad idea.

I moved behind Blaire and placed my hand on her back. She might not realize it, but it showed possession, and these assholes needed to know I was with her. I led the girls over to an empty booth farther away from the dance floor. The music was so damn loud I couldn't hear Blaire's soft voice.

Blaire slid in on one side, and I made sure to stand so that Bethy had no choice but to push me aside or sit across from Blaire. Then I slid in beside Blaire. Bethy didn't miss my move and shot me a glare. She wanted Blaire to hunt for cowboys tonight.

I wasn't going to make that easy. Even if Blaire wanted to,

I wasn't sure I could physically allow her to without beating some ass-wipe's head in.

"What do you want to drink?" I asked, leaning down toward Blaire's ear so she could hear me. And so I could smell her.

"I'm not sure," she said, and glanced over at Bethy "What do I drink?" she asked her.

Bethy looked surprised and laughed. "You haven't been drinking before?"

No, she hadn't been drinking before. Could Bethy not look at Blaire and be able to tell this?

"I'm not old enough to buy my own alcohol. Are you?" she asked sweetly.

I was so glad I was here. The idea of this happening without me here to protect her made me ill.

Bethy clapped her hands like she was giddy with delight at the idea that Blaire was a complete innocent. "This is gonna be so much fun. And yes, I'm twenty-one, or at least my ID says I am." She looked at me. "You need to let her out. I'm taking her to the bar."

Like hell she was. I looked at Blaire, ignoring Bethy. "You've never had alcohol?" I asked, already knowing she hadn't.

"Nope. But I intend to remedy that tonight," she said with determination. Too damn sweet.

"Then you need to go slow. You won't have a very high tolerance," I explained, then turned to grab the arm of the waitress walking past us. I had to feed Blaire first. "We need a menu."

"Why are you ordering food? We're here to drink and dance with cowboys. Not eat," Bethy said angrily.

She could fuck off. I wasn't going to let her hurt Blaire.

Drinking could hurt her if not done right. If Bethy wanted to argue with me, then we were gonna have a problem. "She's never drunk before. She needs to eat first, or she'll be bent over puking her guts out and cursing you in two hours' time."

Bethy waved her hand at me as if I were talking Chinese. "Whatever, Daddy Rush. I'm going to get me somethin' to drink, and I'm getting her somethin', too. So feed her fast."

The waitress was back with the menu, so I took it and turned my attention back to Blaire. "Pick something. No matter what Diva the Drunk says, you need to eat first."

Blaire nodded agreeably. She didn't like the idea of getting sick, either. At least she was cautious. I was thankful for that much. Bethy, not so much. I didn't like her getting close to Bethy.

"The cheese fries look good," Blaire said almost too quietly.

I wasn't going to waste time. Bethy had left for drinks, and I wanted the food in Blaire fast. I motioned the waitress over. "Cheese fries, two orders, and a tall glass of water," I told her.

She nodded and hurried off. I felt better knowing food was coming. And that I was going to watch her eat. It was screwed up that I wanted to watch, but the peanut-butter-sandwich thing was fucking with my head.

"So you're at a honky-tonk. Was it everything you hoped it would be? Because I'll be real honest, this music is painful," I said, leaning back and looking at Blaire. I hadn't really paid attention to the country music since we'd walked inside. I had been more concerned with getting Blaire food.

She shrugged and looked around us. "I just got here, and I haven't drunk or danced yet, so I'll let you know after that happens."

She wanted to dance? Fantastic. "You want to dance?"

"Yes, I do. But I need a shot of courage first, and I need someone to ask me to dance," she said.

"I thought I just asked," I said. I wanted to be the one who held her during those slow country songs. Not some drunk cowboy.

Blaire leaned forward and put her elbows on the table, then propped her chin up on her hands before looking over at me. "You think that's a good idea?"

I didn't have to ask her why she would think it wasn't. We both knew what happened when we touched or got too close. I lost control. She wanted a friend. Nothing more from me. She was smart. "Probably not," I admitted.

She nodded.

The waitress slid the cheese fries in front of us, along with a mug of water that was nice and frosted. Blaire quickly reached for a fry and took a bite.

I couldn't keep from smiling. "That's better than peanut-butter sandwiches, isn't it?" I asked. She grinned and nodded, picking up another fry. I wasn't going to be able to eat. She was too damn fascinating.

"I figured I should start you out easy," Bethy said, sliding back into her side of the booth. "Tequila is a big-girl drink. You're not ready for that yet. This is a lemon drop. It's sweet and yummy."

Shit. She was bringing her shots. What was wrong with beer? Girls always went for those sweet shots and ended up trashed so damn fast. "Eat a few more fries first," I encouraged Blaire.

She didn't argue with me. I watched her eat a couple more,

and then she reached for the lemon drop. "OK, I'm ready," she said, smiling at Bethy. They picked up their drinks together and put them to their lips. I watched as Blaire tipped her head back and drank the too-sweet liquid. She was going to like it. I didn't know how I could handle a drunk Blaire.

"Eat," I said when her eyes met mine over the glass.

She pressed her lips together, and then a giggle broke free. She was laughing at me now. One fucking drink, and she was giggling.

"I met some guys at the bar," Bethy told her while eating her fries. "I pointed you out, and they've been watching us since I sat down. You ready to make a new friend?"

Oh, fuck no. I moved closer to Blaire, fighting the urge to hold her in her seat. She wanted to do this. We were here for her to have a good time.

Blaire nodded and glanced up at me.

"Let her out, Rush. You can keep the booth warm for us in case we come back," Bethy said, sounding annoyed with me again.

I didn't want to do this. She was safe here with me. If I could smell her sweet scent, then that douche watching her could, too. Fuck, I hated this.

Blaire's eyes were hopeful, and I could see she was excited. I couldn't keep her from this. She'd missed so much. Reluctantly, I slid out of the booth and let her out.

"Be careful. I'm here if you need me," I whispered in her ear as she walked past me. She nodded and looked back at me like she might be changing her mind. I'd whisk her out of here so fast. All she had to do was say the word.

"Come on, Blaire. Time to use you to get us free drinks and

men. You are the hottest sidekick I've ever had. This should be fun. Just don't tell these guys you're nineteen. Tell everyone you're twenty-one," Bethy said.

My hands clenched into fists as I sat back down in the now-empty booth.

"OK," Blaire said.

I couldn't watch her go over there. I wouldn't be able to stay away.

I wouldn't look. I wouldn't look.

Ah, hell, I was gonna look. I had started to turn around when a blonde walked over to me and sat down on the table in front of me. "You so don't fit in here," she said, with a Southern drawl that was thicker than usual.

I glanced back at Blaire. She was smiling up at some guy with curls. Fuck. She was happy, though. He wasn't touching her. She looked like she was enjoying herself. I had to let her do this. If I didn't need to drive them home, I would get drunk. It would make this much easier to deal with.

"She yours?" the girl asked, sliding her leg over to dangle beside me.

I turned back to her. "No. She's . . . we're friends," I explained.

The blonde leaned forward, presenting me with a view of her large and very bought-and-paid-for tits.

I was an equal-opportunity kind of guy, so I had no problem with that. Nice tits were nice tits. Hers were nice. I just wasn't interested. I had Blaire to watch out for.

"She's crazy to run off with someone like him when she has someone who looks like you sitting here waiting on her," the girl said, moving her leg closer to me.

I looked back at Blaire, who was talking to the other guy now. Bethy was with the one with the curly hair. Blaire seemed fine. I had to stop watching her. "She's, uh, never been to a bar before. She's exploring things," I said, turning my attention back to the blonde.

The blonde moved her leg up to set her heeled foot on the seat beside me. I glanced down to see a direct view up her skirt. Red panties. Nice.

I slid a finger down her thigh before moving her skirt over so she wasn't flashing me right here where the whole damn bar could see . . . or where Blaire could see.

"Might want to close those," I said, with a smile to ease the rejection.

She laughed and moved to stand up and slide in beside me. "Maybe if I sit here, then you can't keep focusing on your friend, who seems to be enjoying herself just fine. And if I open my legs, no one but you and I can see," she said, leaning toward me so her tits were on display again.

If I could actually get up the desire to play with those toys she was intent on flashing at me, then I might not be so wound up. But not being able to see Blaire was pissing me off. "Look, you're hot. No doubt. But I'm here to keep my friend safe. It's about her," I explained, as my eyes found Blaire walking toward the dance floor with the guy she'd been talking to. His hand was on her back now. Not mine. Jealousy was painful, and I'd never experienced it before. But damn, when it takes hold of you, then you feel it. You fucking know what it is.

"See, she's dancing. Not at all worried about you," the blonde said, pressing closer to me and sliding her hand up my leg.

I reached down and grabbed it before she slid it over my cock. Even if I didn't want to fuck her, my damn cock would react to the attention and give her the wrong idea. I put her hand back in her own lap.

"She has you in all kinds of knots, doesn't she? Damn." The woman looked over at Blaire and shrugged. "Guess that young, fresh thing does it for men. It grows old, though. She won't always be so sweet and new."

She had this all wrong. Most women like her did. They didn't understand that a man could want someone for more than just her looks. That it wasn't always sex that drew them in. That sometimes it was more. More . . .

"I can make you forget she exists," the blonde said, moving her mouth to mine.

"Whoa." I grabbed her head to stop her. I didn't kiss. Not mouths I knew had been on too many cocks to count. "Not going there, sugar. Sorry, but you're right. She has me all kinds of wrapped up. She might not want me that way, but she has my complete attention. No one else is gonna compare."

The woman stuck out her bottom lip in a pout that looked ridiculous, then ran her leg up my side. She wasn't giving up easily. "One kiss. Just one really good kiss," she said, leaning into me again.

I had to hold her body back forcefully this time. "I don't kiss mouths that I know have sucked a cock that isn't mine," I said bluntly, knowing it would stop her.

She froze, and her eyebrows shot up. "You mean you only do virgins?" she asked, incredulous.

I laughed and shook my head. "No. I mean I don't kiss. I fuck, but I don't kiss," I clarified.

She leaned back and looked at me. "Really? And girls are OK with this?"

I had started to respond when I saw that Blaire's date was alone on the dance floor. Fuck! Where was she? "Move," I demanded, shoving the woman back so I could get out of the booth. "Now, dammit, move!" I yelled.

She scrambled backward, glaring at me, but I didn't have time to explain. Blaire was gone, and I didn't see her leave. I was supposed to be watching her. I sucked at this.

I had to find her. Her dance partner started for the door, but some woman walked up to him and distracted him. I'd deal with him later if I needed to. Right now, I was going to see if Blaire had gone outside.

Chapter Seventeen

My heart was pounding so hard that the relief when I saw her standing outside the bar, leaning against the building, made my knees weak. She was here. She was fine.

"Blaire?" I called out to her.

She had her arms crossed over her chest defensively. I wasn't sure what had happened in there, but if the redneck wannabe cowboy had stepped out of line, I was going to rip his arms off.

"Yes," she answered. There was a hesitation to her voice. Something was wrong. She didn't sound like herself.

"I couldn't find you. Why are you out here? This isn't safe."

"I'm fine. Go back inside and continue your make-out session in our booth." She was jealous. Fuck. But I wanted her to be jealous. It made a warmth course through me that felt so wrong, but I couldn't help it. I liked knowing she was jealous. Even though there was nothing for her to be jealous of.

"Why are you out here?" I asked, slowly taking another step toward her.

"Because I want to be," she said, shooting an angry glare in my direction.

"The party is inside. Isn't that what you wanted? A honky-tonk with men and drinks? You're missing it out here." I was trying to lighten the mood. The look on her face said it wasn't working. She was really pissed. All this because she thought I was making out with the blonde in the booth?

"Back off, Rush," she snapped. Well shit, she was mad at me. I hadn't done anything. She'd been the one dancing with the cowboy wannabe.

I took another step toward her. I couldn't see her clearly enough in the darkness. "No. I want to know what happened." She was upset, and I had a hard time believing it was all because of the blonde in the booth with me. There had to be something else.

Blaire put both of her hands on my chest and shoved me. "You want to know what happened? *You* happened, Rush. That's what happened." Her voice verged on a scream. She turned and starting walking away. What the hell?

I reached out and grabbed her before she could go too far. I wasn't letting this one go. She was pissed, and it made no fucking sense. All this anger, even though she'd seen me with other women. She had been dancing with another guy just minutes before. Had it all changed for her, too? Was this not just all me now? Because if she wanted more, then I wasn't going to be able to say no. I was past that. "What does that mean, Blaire?" I asked, pulling her back up against my chest.

She squirmed in my arms, making frustrated little growls. "Let. Me. Go," she demanded.

Not a chance. "Not until you tell me what your problem is," I said. She began to twist and fight against me harder, but I held on to her easily enough. I didn't want to hurt her, but I needed to understand what was wrong. Either I'd pissed her off or that guy in the bar had.

"I don't like seeing you touch other women. And when other men grope my ass, I hate it. I want it to be you touching me there. Wanting to touch me there. But you don't, and I have to deal with it. Now, let me go!"

I hadn't been expecting that. She took advantage of the fact that she'd just surprised the hell out of me and jerked free from my hold, then took off running. I wasn't sure where she thought she was going in the dark by herself.

She wanted me to touch her . . . there. Shit. I was sunk. I couldn't fight this. I needed to. If I wanted to save us both pain later, I could turn around and go back inside. But damn, I couldn't find the strength to fight this need. I wanted her. I wanted her so fucking badly I was ready to make this work. Denying myself was one thing, but denying Blaire was a whole other issue.

I didn't think about it. I couldn't. I just acted on instinct.

I went after her.

Once I was close enough to the Range Rover, I clicked the unlock button. I was touching her tonight. Right now. Right fucking now. And it was the stupidest thing I could do. For both of us. But I just didn't give a shit anymore. I was taking what I wanted. What she wanted.

"Get in, or I'll put you in," I demanded.

Her eyes went wide with shock, and she scrambled quickly into the backseat. Her sweet little ass was stuck up in the air, and my dick was instantly hard. God, why did I want her so badly? I shouldn't do this. Blaire was the one person I couldn't have. She knew nothing about Nan and her dad and me. This would all end up destroying me. Or maybe it wouldn't. Maybe she would listen to me. Understand all of this.

I climbed in behind her.

"What are you doing?" she asked.

I didn't answer, because I wasn't fucking sure. I pressed her up against the seat and took another taste. The innocence pouring off her was intoxicating. She was pure. Not just with her body but with her thoughts. She wasn't spiteful. She didn't seek revenge. She trusted me. I was the world's biggest dick.

I grabbed her hips and moved her so that I could settle between her legs. I needed the connection. The warmth. Blaire didn't fight me but did exactly as I prompted. I wanted to claim her. Completely. But it was wrong. Too much stood between us. Things she'd never forgive. Things she would never understand. Frantic, I reached for the hem of her shirt.

"Take it off," I said, as I lifted it over her head and threw it into the front seat. The soft, perfect skin of her breasts peeked out of the top of the lacy bra she was wearing. I needed to see it all. I wanted to taste it all. "I want it all off, sweet Blaire." I reached for the bra clasp and quickly undid it, then slid the bra down her arms. She was beautiful. I'd known she would be. But seeing the hard pink nipples against her creamy, smooth skin made me realize I wouldn't be able to go back. "This is why I tried to stay away. This, Blaire. I won't be able to stop this. Not now."

When someone is handed a piece of heaven, he can't just forget it. My breathing was becoming difficult as I pulled her closer and lowered my head to pull one of those nipples into my mouth and sucked on it, as I'd imagined doing more than once.

Blaire grabbed my shoulders and cried out my name, making any control I had thought I was holding on to vanish. I let her nipple pop free of my mouth so I could stick my tongue out and let her see the silver barbell she'd been so interested in flick over her skin. "Tastes like candy. Girls shouldn't taste so sweet. It's dangerous," I told her, then ran my nose along her neck and inhaled deeply. "And you smell incredible."

Nothing would ever smell as good as Blaire. Nothing. Her mouth was slightly open, and she took fast little breaths as I cupped her breasts with my hands. That mouth and those lips. I couldn't get them out of my head. Kissing had always been something I didn't do easily. But with Blaire, it was all I could think about. She tasted so sweet and clean. Her mouth was mine and only mine when I kissed her lips.

Tugging on her nipples, I teased her, and she moaned into my mouth. Her small hands slipped under my shirt and began exploring my stomach. She was spending a lot of time on my abs, causing a smile to tug at my lips. My girl liked my stomach. I'd give her better access if that was what she wanted.

I reached for my shirt with one hand, jerked it over my head, and tossed it away, then went right back to kissing those now-swollen lips of hers. I loved the way they felt against mine.

Blaire arched her back, rubbing her breasts against my now-bare chest, and I had to suck in to catch my breath. Shit, that felt good. It was so simple, but it was incredible, because it was Blaire. Everything with her felt like it was new. I didn't want to miss any of it. I wanted to soak in every moan and cry from her lips.

I wrapped her up in my arms and pressed her against me, and she clawed gently at my back as an excited sound came from her mouth.

"Sweet Blaire," I said, and I freed her mouth long enough to pull her bottom lip into my mouth so I could suck on it. I loved how full it was. I could spend hours with just her mouth. But she was wiggling under me and opening her legs wider. She was searching, and I knew exactly what she wanted, even if she wasn't sure.

I wanted to take my time and cherish her, but her sexy little body was getting needy and moving frantically beneath me. I touched her knee, and she jumped from my touch and then stilled. Slowly, I ran my hand up her thigh, giving her time to stop me if this was too fast.

Her legs fell open completely, as if offering me an invitation, and the smell of her heat hit me. Holy shit, that was good. So so so good. I inhaled deeply before running a finger along the wet fabric of her panties.

Blaire jerked against my touch and let out a small whimper. God, how was I gonna be able to control myself? This was too much. She smelled too good, and her sounds . . . fuck, they were hot.

"Easy. I just want to see if it's as fucking sweet down there as the rest of you," I told her, and she trembled in my arms. She didn't want me to stop. The trembling and the desperate look in her eyes let me know everything I needed to know. I held her gaze and my breath as I slipped a finger inside the satin and felt the wetness there, waiting for me.

"Rush," she said in a desperate voice as she squeezed my shoulder.

"Shhh, it's OK," I said.

But was it? Fuck, she was soaked, and the smell was intoxicating. The whole damn car smelled like Blaire's arousal. I was so close to coming in my jeans it was ridiculous. She hadn't even touched me.

I buried my head in her neck and tried to smell the sweet scent of her skin and get some control. Her arousal was about to kill me. "This is too fucking much," I told her.

Then I moved my finger through her hot, slick opening, and she bucked underneath me and screamed out my name. Shit. Oh, fuck. Shit. I was panting. I couldn't catch my breath. I moved my finger and slid into the tightness waiting for me, and her body squeezed me, sucking my finger in.

"Shit. Mother*fucking* hell. Wet, hot . . . so fucking hot. And Jesus, you're so tight." My words sounded as out of control as I felt. Nothing should be this fucking amazing.

"Rush. Please," she begged me. "I need . . ." She didn't finish her thought, because she was so damn innocent she didn't know what she needed. God, she had me. That was it. She had me. I couldn't let her go. Not now. I was owned.

I pressed a kiss to her chin, as she threw her head back and arched into me. "I know what you need. I'm just not sure I can handle watching you get it. You've got me all kinds of worked up, girl. I'm trying hard to be a good boy. I can't lose control in the back of a damn car."

She shook her head frantically. "Please, don't be good. Please."

Fuck me. "Shit, baby. Stop it. I'm going to explode. I'll give you your release, but when I finally bury myself inside you for the first time, you won't be sprawled in the back of my car. You'll be in my bed." I would not take her in the back of this car. She was too damn precious for that.

I moved my hand and slid my thumb over her clit to rub it gently as I slipped my finger in and out of her greedy entrance. She began clawing at me and panting my name. The begging was about to kill me. All I could think about was what it would feel like to be buried up inside this heaven and have her begging me for release. Fuck, I was gonna come.

"That's it. Come for me, sweet Blaire. Come on my hand, and let me feel it. I want to watch you." I wasn't sure if she even understood what I was asking her for, but I couldn't be quiet.

"RUUUUUSH!" She cried out my name and began riding my hand as she jerked and trembled. Her hands grasped for me like she thought she was falling. I held her as she chanted my name. My world exploded, and I bent my head to breathe her in as I shuddered, unable to believe what had just happened.

"Ahhhh, yeah. That's it. Fuck, yes. You're so beautiful," I told her, as I let the waves of pleasure wash over me. She began to ease her hold on me as a sweet, lethargic smile touched her lips. I removed my hand from between her legs and enjoyed her smell before slipping my finger into my mouth and tasting her.

She tasted even better than I'd expected. Was that even fucking possible?

Blaire's eyelashes fluttered, and she opened her eyes to look up at me.

I could see the moment she realized exactly why I had my finger in my mouth. The shocked look was followed by pink cheeks. She had just screamed my name and come apart in my lap, but the sight of me sucking her off my finger made her blush.

"I was right. You're just as sweet in that hot little pussy of yours as you are everywhere else," I told her, just to see if her eyes could get any bigger.

She closed them tightly, unable to look at me.

I started laughing. She was perfect. "Oh, come on, sweet Blaire. You just came wild and sexy all over my hand and even left some claw marks on my back to prove it. Don't go getting shy on me now. 'Cause, baby, before the night is over, you will be naked in my bed." And I meant that. I wanted her in my bed. And if this could possibly get any better, I wouldn't let her out.

She peeked back up at me, and the interest in her eyes made me bite back a groan. I would not do anything else in this damn car. She was too good for a car. I wanted to give her the best of everything. That included the best of sex.

"Let me get you dressed, then I'll go find Bethy and see if she needs a ride or if she found a cowboy to take her home," I said.

She stretched her body out like a cat, and I clenched my fists to keep from grabbing her and claiming her mouth again. "OK," she agreed.

"If I wasn't hard as a damn rock right now, I'd consider staying right here and enjoying the sleepy little pleased look in your eyes. I like knowing I put it there. But I need some more," I whispered against her ear.

She tensed, then eased back against me. Damn, I had to get her clothes on her—and fast.

Chapter Eighteen

I reached for her bra and concentrated on dressing her. I pressed a kiss to her shoulder before I covered it up with her shirt. She had let me put her bra and shirt back on without protest, and the caveman in me was beating on his chest. I loved taking care of her, and having her let me only made me a little more insane where she was concerned.

"I'd prefer you stay out here while I go find Bethy. You have that well-pleased look on your face, and it's seriously sexy. I don't want to end up in a fight," I told her once I had her covered up again.

"I came here with Bethy because I was trying to encourage her not to sleep around with guys who would never look at her for more than a fun time. Then you came with us, and now here I am in the backseat of your car. I feel like I owe her an explanation," she said, looking worried.

I had assumed Bethy had been trying to ruin Blaire, but Blaire had been the one to reach out to Bethy. Interesting. My sweet Blaire was trying to save the world from itself. No one had ever saved her. Until now. Damn time someone showed her how special she was.

She was watching me nervously. Did she think she had just

done what she was trying to stop Bethy from doing? Surely she understood this was different.

"I'm trying to decide if you meant that to sound like you were doing what you encouraged her not to do," I said, as I moved over her and slid a hand into her hair. "Because I've had a taste, and I'm not sharing. This isn't just for fun. I may be slightly addicted." This was nothing like what she was trying to stop Bethy from doing. I would have never touched Blaire had I not been sure I was claiming her as mine. There would be no one else touching her.

I leaned down and kissed those lips I loved so much. Tasting her bottom lip with the top of my tongue had become one of my favorite things to do. She always shivered when I did it, and the taste was always delicious.

"Mmmmm, yeah. You stay here. I'll get Bethy to come out and talk to you," I whispered against her mouth.

She nodded but didn't say anything else.

I moved away from her warmth and opened the door to get out. I had to find Bethy and get us home. I wanted Blaire in my room. In my bed. I wanted more of what we'd just had. I could fix the past. I could make it all right. I would make it right for Blaire. I had to. I couldn't lose this.

Back in the bar, I looked around and found Bethy with some guy, taking a shot of something that didn't look like another girlie drink. Great. I didn't want a drunk Bethy to hinder my plans. Blaire couldn't fix what had been messed up for years. Once Bethy had been different. I remembered her when she was younger. I'd seen her with Tripp once. They had been friends, I think, but then he'd run off, and the next time I saw Bethy was underneath a guy whose daddy owned condos along the Gulf coast. She'd been fucking the trust-fund brats ever since.

Her gaze landed on me, and I motioned for her to meet me outside, then turned and went back out into the night. I looked in the direction of my Range Rover and made sure Blaire was still safely inside.

"You two disappeared," Bethy said, with a slur to her voice and a big grin on her face. I turned to see her walking toward me. Then she stumbled, and I had to reach out and grab her before she face-planted on the pavement. "Oops." She giggled, going limp in my arms. "I can't feel my feet," she said through her laughter.

I wasn't going to be able to leave her here. "Looks like I'm taking you home now, too," I told her, and stood her up straight.

"What? No no no no. I dunwanna go yet," she said, shaking a finger in my direction. "Blaire needs to come see the new cowboys I found. She'll love 'em."

I tensed and jerked her toward the car. "Blaire isn't interested in cowboys anymore. Got that? No more guys for Blaire. She's going home with me," I said angrily.

Bethy stopped and swayed, then looked at me, her eyes round with understanding. "She lives at your house. Do you mean home to *her* room or home to *your* room?" she asked, then burped and covered her mouth.

"My room. Go," I said, making her walk again.

"Oh, shit," Bethy said in a loud attempt at a whisper. "You—oh, shit, Rush, you can't fuck her. She ain't . . . I think she's a virgin." Bethy was whispering loudly enough for the entire parking lot to hear her.

"Shut up, Bethy," I growled, and opened the car door for her. "She wants to go home, with me. But first, she wants to talk to you." This was not how I wanted to spend the drive back to Rosemary Beach. I'd hoped I could talk to Blaire. Now we had a drunk Bethy talking about Blaire's virginity. Shit.

"Well, look at you. Making it with the hottest thing in Rosemary Beach in the back of his Range Rover. And here I thought you wanted a blue-collar man," Bethy said to Blaire.

"Climb on in, Bethy, before you fall on your ass out here," I ordered, wishing I could shut her the hell up.

"I don't wanna leave. I liked Earl, or was his name Kevin? No, wait, what happened to Nash? I lost him . . . I think," Bethy muttered, as she climbed inside clumsily.

"Who are Earl and Kevin?" Blaire asked.

Bethy reached for something to grab, then fell backward onto the seat and almost on top of Blaire. "Earl is married. He said he wasn't, but he is. I could tell. The married ones always have the smell about 'em."

I closed Bethy's door and then walked around to get Blaire out of the backseat. She was going up front with me. I jerked her door open and held out my hand for hers. "Don't try to make sense of anything she says. I found her at the bar finishing up a round of six tequila shots that married Earl had bought her. She's trashed." I wanted to clear up anything Bethy had said or was going to say that could upset Blaire.

Blaire slipped her hand into mine, and I squeezed it to reassure her.

"No need in explaining anything to her tonight. She won't remember it in the morning," I told Blaire.

She was worried about clearing the air with Bethy, and Bethy was doing exactly what she always did—just without the trust-funders.

I helped Blaire down, then pulled her against me and closed the door, leaving Bethy inside. "I want a taste of those sweet lips, but I'm going to deny myself. We need to get her home before she gets sick," I said, not wanting this to spoil what had just happened with us.

Blaire nodded, staring up at me with those trusting eyes. I didn't want to ever let that face down.

"But what I said earlier. I meant it. I want you in my bed tonight," I reminded her, in case it was possible she could have forgotten.

She nodded again. I slipped my hand to her lower back and walked her over to the passenger door. I wasn't going to pretend we were friends anymore. We weren't friends. We had never been friends. It was more than that. With Blaire, it was always more.

"Fuck the friend thing," I told her, before taking her waist and picking her up to put her in the seat. It was high, and I wanted a reason to touch her. I closed her door and walked around to climb in, and the grin on her face made me warm inside. "What's the grin for?" I asked, hoping I had put it there.

She shrugged and bit her bottom lip. "'Fuck the friend thing.' It made me laugh."

I laughed. Good, I had put that smile there. I'd also made her laugh. Why did it feel like I'd just solved world hunger?

"I know something you don't know. Yes, I do. Yes, I do," Bethy began chanting in a drunken singsong voice.

I didn't want her distracting us. Messing this up. It was my time with Blaire, and I wanted that. Why couldn't she just pass out or something?

Blaire shifted in her seat to look back at Bethy.

"I know something," Bethy whispered loudly like she had been doing outside.

"I heard that," Blaire said.

"It's a big secret. A huge one . . . and I know it. I'm not supposed to, but I do. I know something you don't know. You don't know. You don't know." Bethy started singing again.

She knew a secret. A sick knot formed in my stomach. I had secrets. Did she know my secrets? Did she know what Blaire didn't know? How could I have Blaire if Bethy told her before I could fix it? "That's enough, Bethy," I warned.

Blaire turned back around, and I could tell I had startled her. I just wanted Bethy to shut up. I didn't want to hear any secrets she knew. I reached over and slipped a hand over Blaire's. I needed to reassure her, but I couldn't look at her right now. The panic in my throat was taking over.

Bethy couldn't know. Could she? No one knew. Had Nan told someone? Fuck. I couldn't let this get out. I had to make this right. Blaire needed me. I couldn't lose her.

"That was the best time ever. I like blue-collar fellas. They're so much fun." Bethy started babbling again. "You should have looked around some more, Blaire. It would have been smarter on your part. Rush is a bad idea. 'Cause there is always Nan."

Motherfuckinghell!

She knew something. *No.* She couldn't know. Not the truth. I moved my hand from Blaire's to grip the steering wheel. I needed to think, and throwing Bethy's drunk ass out of the car wasn't an option. Blaire would never forgive me for that.

"Is Nan your sister?" Blaire asked. The confusion in her voice made me wince. She was questioning my relationship with Nan. If she only knew the truth. I wouldn't have her. She wouldn't be here.

I just nodded. I couldn't say anything else. My throat was thick.

"What did Bethy mean, then? How would us sleeping together affect Nan?"

How did I respond to that? I didn't know what Bethy knew exactly, but I couldn't tell Blaire the truth. I hadn't figured out how to make the past OK. How to make Blaire not leave me when she found out the truth.

She was going to keep asking me questions. I had to stop her. I couldn't tell her anything. Not now.

"Nan is my younger sister. I won't . . . I can't talk about her with you."

Blaire's body was rigid. The tension in the car was over-powering. There had to be a way out of this. Blaire trusted me. I wanted that trust. I wanted to deserve it. Bethy couldn't know. She wouldn't know. Nan had never said anything to anyone. It was a secret she held close. I was overreacting.

Bethy's snoring filled the car, and Blaire fixed her gaze on the road. Neither of us said anything. I didn't want Bethy to wake up and say anything. She was better off passed out. I was safer that way. My secrets were safer.

The distance between Blaire and me seemed to grow by the second, and I hated it. I wanted her in my arms again. I wanted her crying out my name. I didn't want this wall between us.

When I pulled up to the office, I didn't ask Blaire if this was where we needed to leave Bethy. I couldn't say anything to her. I was terrified she'd know. Had she sat there and figured it all out?

I shook Bethy enough to wake her up and help her out of the car. She began mumbling that her dad would kill her and she wanted to sleep in the office. I was pretty sure her aunt Darla would kick her ass in the morning, but that wasn't my problem. I fished out the key from Bethy's purse and unlocked the door, then got her inside.

The large leather sofa was close to the door, thank God, because Bethy reeked of cheap tequila, and I didn't want to be the one holding her up when she started puking. I dropped her onto the sofa. "Lie down," I instructed her. I grabbed the nearest trash can and set it beside her head. "Vomit in this. You get that shit on the floor, and Darla will be even more pissed."

Bethy groaned and rolled over.

I went to leave. Just as I opened the door, Bethy's voice stopped me.

"I won't tell her about Nan's daddy. But you need to." She looked sad as her glassy eyes met mine. She knew who Nan's daddy was. Shit.

"I will. When it's time," I told her.

"Don't wait too long," she said, then closed her eyes. Her mouth fell open with a soft snore.

I locked the door and closed it tightly behind me. She was right. I had to fix this before it was too late.

Chapter Nineteen

Your room is upstairs now," I reminded her once we had stepped inside the house and she headed for the kitchen. We still hadn't spoken. I wasn't sure what to say to her or even how to talk to her now.

She paused, then turned and headed for the stairs. I couldn't just let her go like this.

"I tried to stay away from you," I said.

She stopped and turned to look down at me. The hurt in her eyes was too much. I didn't want to hurt her. Yet I would be her biggest heartbreak. I hated myself. I hated what I was, who I was.

"That first night, I tried to get rid of you. Not because I disliked you." I laughed bitterly at the truth. "But because I knew. I *knew* you'd get under my skin. I knew I wouldn't be able to stay away. Maybe I hated you a little bit then because of the weakness you'd be able to find in me." I had known from the first moment that she was trouble. She'd break me. But I hadn't known she'd own me.

"What is so wrong with you being attracted to me?" she asked, a tear glistening in the corner of her eye. Shit. I hated knowing she didn't understand.

"Because you don't know everything, and I can't tell you. I

can't tell you Nan's secrets. They're hers. I love her, Blaire. I've loved her and protected her all my life. She's my little sister. It's what I do. Even though I want you like I've never wanted anything in my life, I can't tell you Nan's secrets." If she could just take that as her answer and give me time. All the things I'd done had to be fixed. There had to be a way to right the wrongs.

"I can understand that. It's OK. I shouldn't have asked. I'm sorry," she said in a soft voice. She meant that. She was fucking apologizing. To me. "Good night, Rush," she said, and turned and left me there.

I let her go. She was telling me it was OK to have my secrets but that I couldn't have her, too. How would I do this? I had tasted her in my arms. I knew what her smile could do to me and how the way she looked at me controlled my fucking moods. It was like she'd become the sun, and I'd started revolving around her. She was my center.

Yet I was the reason she had lived through hell. I had given her father a place to run to. I had gone to him when he was weak and needed to be with his daughter and his wife. I'd given him somewhere else to go. Another life to walk into. Another daughter to claim and another family to belong to.

And he'd left her. All alone. If I had just cared enough to find out who I was taking him from . . . but I hadn't cared. I had just wanted to give Nan what she wanted so badly. I hadn't thought of anyone else. Only Nan. It was always Nan.

Or it had been. It wasn't anymore.

I couldn't ignore the truth. Blaire's happiness and safety meant too much to me. Protecting Nan was no longer my number one priority. Blaire was taking that spot. She had moved right into my life and changed it all. I should hate her for that. But I couldn't. I would never hate her. That was impossible.

I climbed the stairs and stopped at the door to the bedroom where she was now tucked away. I had wanted her in my bed tonight. But knowing that she was in sleeping in luxury meant I would be able to rest easier. The regret in my chest would be my only companion in bed tonight.

The sound of a phone ringing broke through the sweet darkness, and I forced my eyes open to reach for the offending sound. I had lain awake most of the night. Of course, now that I'd finally fallen asleep, my damn phone had to ring. Grabbing it, I noticed the sun through the blinds. It was later than I thought. Maybe I had been asleep for longer than I'd thought.

"Hello," I snarled into the phone.

"Are you still asleep?" Woods's annoying voice didn't put me in a better mood.

"What do you want?" I asked. It was none of his business if I was still asleep.

"It's about your sister," he said.

I sat up in bed and rubbed the sleep from my eyes. I wasn't in the mood to wake up and deal with Nan's problems. I had my own. "What?" I barked.

"If she speaks to Blaire or any of my other employees with disrespect, I'll make sure her membership is pulled. You may not care that she's a spoiled brat, but when her venom causes a scene and embarrasses the best server we've had in the dining room in months, then it becomes an issue."

Blaire? What? "What are you saying? Did Nan do some-thing to Blaire? Or one of your servers? I'm confused."

"Blaire is one of my servers. I moved her to the dining room last week. And your bitch of a sister called her white trash and demanded that I fire her today. In front of everyone." Woods's voice was getting louder. He was pissed but nothing close to the level of angry I was dealing with. "I realize you don't care about Blaire. It's obvious from the fact that she's sleeping in your damn pantry. But she's special. She works hard, and ev-eryone loves her. I won't allow Nan to hurt her. Do you un-derstand me?"

I didn't like Woods saying that Blaire was special. I fuck-ing knew she was special, and he needed to back the hell off. And why had he moved her inside from the golf course? Had he wanted her near him? Was that it? As much as I wanted to be relieved that she was out of the heat, the idea that he had moved her inside to be near him infuriated me. And Nan. Fuck. She'd pushed me too far. I was going to have to deal with her. I wasn't OK with her talking to Blaire that way, either. No one was going to call Blaire names. Ever. Another problem I had to fix. Yet another thing that was my fault.

"Do. You. Understand. Me." Woods's voice reminded me that I hadn't responded to him. If it weren't for the fact that he was angry over how Blaire was treated, I would remind him exactly who he was talking to. But just this once, I was going to allow him to be angry at me. Because he was right. This was my fault. I'd created the monster my sister had turned into.

"She isn't in the pantry anymore. I moved her to a bed-room. I'll deal with Nan," I told him, then decided he needed to understand something else, too. "Blaire is mine. Don't touch her. I will kill you. Do you understand me?"

Woods let out a humorless laugh. "Yeah. Whatever, Finlay. I'm not scared of your threats. The only reason I'm not touching Blaire is that she doesn't want me. It's fucking obvious who she wants. So calm the hell down. You've had her from the beginning. You sure as hell don't deserve her, though," he said, and then the call ended.

Woods thought she wanted me. God, I hoped he was right.

I stood up and called Nan.

"Hello," she said in an annoyed tone.

"Where are you?" I asked as I headed for the bathroom.

"The club. I'm playing tennis in ten minutes," she replied.

It would take me thirty minutes to take my shower and get some coffee in me. "My house, thirty minutes," I said, and hung up, not waiting for her to argue. She knew not to piss me off, and I had no doubt she knew exactly what this was about.

I would make sure my sister left Blaire alone. Then I was going to get Blaire a phone. She needed a damn cell phone. I wanted to make sure she was OK when I didn't know where she was.

And I was going to cook for her. I wanted to watch her eat. I wanted to feed her. Make up for how badly I'd fucked things up before.

I also didn't want her sleeping in that bedroom tonight. I wanted her in mine.

Chapter Twenty

I was standing on the balcony when I heard Nan's voice from inside. "Where are you?" she called out. She wasn't happy about being here. Good. She really wasn't going to be happy about it when I was done with her.

I walked inside as she came into the living room wearing her tennis skirt and looking pissed off. I was expecting her to be angry, but it pissed me off that she thought she had the right to be. After the way she had treated Blaire, did she think I wouldn't call her out on it?

"You ruined my plans. This better be good," she snapped.

I set my coffee cup down on the nearest table and turned to look at my sister. "Let me get something straight, because you must need reminding. Unless you want to get a job and pay for all your shit, then I have a say in how you act. I've let you act like a brat most of your life because I love you. I know that life with Mom was unfair for you. But I will not . . ." I paused and took a step toward her and leveled my gaze on her so she could see just how serious I was. "*I will not* allow you to hurt Blaire. Ever. She has done nothing to you. You blame her for the sorry excuse for a father you have. Blaire is a victim of that man just as much as you are. So do not speak to her like you did today ever again. I swear, Nan, I love you, but I won't let you hurt her. Do not test me."

Nan's eyes went wide with surprise, and the fake tears I was used to her springing on me immediately glistened in her eyes. "You're choosing her over me. Are you . . . are you fucking her? That's it, isn't it? That little slut!"

I was in her face so fast that she stumbled backward. I reached out and grabbed her arm to keep her from falling and jerked her back up. "Don't you say it. I swear to God, Nan, you are going to push me too far. Think before you speak."

She sniffled and let the tears she could turn on like a damn faucet roll down her face. I hated making her cry. The sick knot I got in my stomach when someone hurt Nan was forming. "I'm . . . I'm your sister. How could you do this to me? I was . . . You know what she did? Who she is? She kept him from me! My father, Rush. I've lived this life because I didn't have him." She was sobbing now and shaking her head, as if she couldn't believe I could forget all this.

She would never see the truth. She was determined to blame and hate someone, but she refused to hate the person who deserved it the most. "Blaire was a child. She did nothing to you. She couldn't help that she was born. She had no clue you even existed. Why can't you see that? Why can't you see the kind, honest, giving, hardworking person your sister is? No one can hate her! She's fucking perfect!"

"Don't you . . ." She pointed her finger at me, with horror on her face. "*Do not call her my sister!*" she screamed hysterically.

Sighing, I sat down on the sofa and held my head in my

hands. Nan was so stubborn. "Nan, you share a father. That makes her your sister," I reminded her.

"No. I don't care. I do not care. I hate her. She's manipulative, and she's fake. She's using sex to control you."

I shot back up out of my seat. "I haven't fucked her, so don't say that! Stop accusing her of shit you know nothing about. Blaire isn't a whore. She's a virgin, Nan. A virgin. You want to know why she's a virgin? Because she spent her teen years taking care of her sick mother while running the household and going to school. She had no time to be a kid. She had no time to sow any wild oats. She was abandoned by her father for *you*. So if anyone should hate someone, *she* should hate *you*."

Nan straightened her spine, her tears now dry. Which made this easier on me. I was all Nan had in the world, and I knew that. I didn't want her thinking I had abandoned her. She was always going to be my little sister. But she was an adult now, and it was time she started acting like one. "And you. She should hate you, too," Nan said, then turned and headed for the door. I didn't call her back. I was too exhausted to deal with her any more today. I trusted she would leave Blaire alone for now.

I spent the rest of the day pushing Nan's words from my head. I focused on getting Blaire a phone and then buying the things that I needed to make her a meal. A good one. Something to impress her and get her to talk to me. To forgive me for completely shutting down on her last night.

I knew she wouldn't accept the phone from me, so I left a

note in her truck telling her it was from her dad. I hated giving that stupid fucker any credit, but I wanted Blaire to take the phone. I needed her to have a phone for my sanity. If I was going to keep her safe, then she needed it.

Glancing at the time, I realized she was more than likely in her truck by now. I picked up my phone and pressed her number, which I had saved in my phone.

"Hello," she said softly. I could hear the confusion in her voice. Had she not read the note?

"I see you got the phone. Do you like it?" I asked.

"Yes, it's really nice. But why did Dad want me to have it?" she asked. That was why she was confused. She didn't expect the selfish bastard to do anything for her like this. She wasn't an idiot.

"Safety measure. All females need a phone. Especially ones who drive vehicles older than they are. You could break down at any moment," I replied, deciding that I would tell her why I wanted her to have a phone instead.

"I have a gun," she said, with determination in her voice.

She was so sure she could take care of herself. "Yeah, you do, badass. But a gun can't tow your truck." There, let her argue with that. "Are you coming home?" I asked. I hadn't thought about the fact that she might have plans tonight when I'd decided to cook her a meal and set up a seduction scene.

"Yes, if that's OK. I can go do something else if you need me to stay away," she replied. She still didn't get it. She thought I wanted her to stay away. That there was anything else in the world I would rather do than be near her.

"No. I want you here. I cooked," I said.

She paused, and I heard a surprised little intake of breath

that made me smile. "Oh. OK. Well, I'll be there in a few minutes."

"See you soon," I said, and I ended the call before she heard me laugh from pure fucking happiness. She was coming home. Here. To spend the night with me. I was fixing this. I was going to find a way to make her understand. I couldn't lose her.

I went back to my food preparation. I didn't cook for people often. Mostly just myself, when I really wanted something. Being able to cook something for Blaire was different. I enjoyed every damn minute of it.

She wasn't used to being taken care of or pampered, and that was a damn shame. Blaire was the kind of female who should be cherished. I opened the fridge, pulled out a Corona and opened it, then sliced a lime and put it on the rim. Most girls I knew liked lime with their Coronas. I wasn't sure Blaire was going to like beer, but I was making Mexican food, and you had to have a Corona with this meal.

I fixed the cheese, chicken, and vegetable mixture inside the flour tortillas, then placed them on the hot skillet.

"Smells good." Blaire's voice broke into my thoughts.

I glanced over my shoulder to see her dressed in the server uniform from the club. Her blond hair was pulled back in a ponytail, but there was a small smile tugging on her lips. She'd caught me humming along to one of my dad's newest songs.

"It is," I assured her, then wiped my hands on a towel and went to pick up the Corona I had fixed for her. "Here, drink up. The enchiladas are almost finished. I need to flip the quesadillas, and they need a few more minutes. We should be ready to eat soon."

She took the beer and slowly put it to her lips. This was her first time with beer. She didn't spit it out, which was a good sign.

"I'm hoping you eat Mexican," I said, as I pulled the enchiladas out of the oven. What I really hoped was that this was good. I hadn't made enchiladas in a while. I even had to Google some recipes to make sure I got it right.

"I love Mexican food," she said, still smiling. "I will admit I'm really impressed that you can cook it."

Good. I wanted to impress her tonight. Convince her that I wasn't an asshole. I looked up at her and winked. "I got all kinds of talents that would blow your mind."

Her cheeks flushed, and she took a larger gulp of the Corona. I was making her nervous. I didn't mean to do that. It was easy to forget that Blaire wasn't used to flirting.

"Easy, girl. You gotta eat something, too. When I said drink up, I didn't mean for you to gulp it down," I told her, not wanting her to get drunk or sick.

She nodded and wiped the drop of beer that had clung to her lips.

All I could think about was licking it off for her. How plump and smooth her bottom lip felt under my tongue. I had to look away. My food was going to fucking burn.

I had already made the tacos and burritos, so I moved the quesadillas to the platter I had put the others on. There was no way we were going to eat all this. I'd gone overboard, but I wasn't sure what she liked, and I wanted her to enjoy her meal. My need to watch her eat was quickly feeling like an addiction.

"Everything else is on the table already. Grab me a Corona

out of the fridge, and follow me," I told her, moving to the table with the platter. I headed for the balcony outside. At first, I had disliked this idea, because she'd seen me out here once before on a date, and I didn't want that image in her head. But the waves and the Gulf breeze made everything seem more intimate. I just hoped she wasn't thinking about me fucking another woman the whole time we were out here.

"Sit. I'll fix your plate," I said.

She nodded and sat on the chair nearest to the door. I could see the surprise in her eyes, and I liked that this wasn't something she expected. I wanted her thoughts on us. No one else. My past was just that—my past. Besides, if she only knew just who I'd been fantasizing about that night when I'd been on this porch with Anya . . .

I fixed her plate and set it down in front of her. Then I leaned down to her ear so I could smell her, because it was driving me crazy. "Can I get you another drink?" I asked, needing a reason for inhaling her neck.

She shook her head no.

I forced myself to move to the other side of the table. I fixed my plate and looked up at her. "If you hate it, don't tell me. My ego can't handle it."

She took a bite of the enchilada. The flicker in her eyes told me she was pleased. I felt like sighing in relief. I hadn't fucked it up. "It's delicious, and I can't say I'm surprised," she told me.

I decided to try it out myself. Grinning, I started eating and watched as she relaxed and took another drink of her beer before eating some more. Each time she took a bite, I fought the urge to stop and watch. It was sick, really. She was just fucking eating. Why was I so completely obsessed with her eating? It had to be the peanut butter's fault. I wasn't going to get over that anytime soon.

We ate in silence. I didn't want to interrupt her, since she looked like she was enjoying herself. When she leaned back and took a long drink from her bottle, then set it down, I knew she was finished.

"I'm sorry about how Nan treated you today," I told her. It wasn't enough. Nan owed her an apology, but nothing I could do would get her an apology from Nan.

"How did you know about that?" Blaire asked, shifting nervously in her seat.

"Woods called me. He was warning me that Nan would be asked to leave the next time she was rude to an employee," I explained. I hated making him look like a damn hero, but it was the truth, and I wasn't going to add any lies to the ones already between us.

Blaire nodded. She didn't seem overly impressed, which was good. I didn't like her having any feelings at all where Woods was concerned.

"She shouldn't have spoken to you that way. I've had a talk with her. She promised me it wouldn't happen again. But if it does somewhere else, then please come tell me," I told her, which wasn't the exact truth. Nan had promised me nothing. But my warning had been enough. I knew that.

Disappointment flashed in Blaire's eyes, and she stood up. "Thank you. I appreciate the gesture. It was very nice of you. I assure you that I don't intend to tattle to Woods if Nan is rude to me in the future. He just happened to witness it firsthand today." She picked up her drink. "Dinner was lovely. Nice to have after a long day at work. Thank you so much." She wouldn't look at me as she turned and hurried inside.

Shit. What did I say wrong? I stood up and followed her inside. Tonight was not ending like this. I was going crazy. Blaire had to stop throwing me so completely off my tracks. I did this as an apology because of my asshole behavior last night and because I wanted to do something for her. Take care of her.

She was washing off her plate in the sink, and the slump in her shoulders broke me.

"Blaire," I said, caging her body against the counter. Her smell filled my head, and I had to close my eyes to keep from getting light-headed. Fuck, that was good. "This wasn't an attempt to apologize for Nan. It was an attempt to apologize for me. I'm sorry about last night. I lay in bed all night wishing you were there with me. Wishing I hadn't pushed you away. I push people away, Blaire. It's a protective mechanism for me. But I don't want to push you away." I didn't know how else to explain this to her.

She leaned back against me some, and I took that as my green light.

I moved away the hair brushing her shoulder and pressed a kiss to the warm, soft skin there. "Please. Forgive me. One more chance, Blaire. I want this. I want you."

She let out a deep breath, then turned to face me. Her arms went up and wrapped around my neck. Those beautiful blue eyes of her locked on mine. "I'll forgive you on one condition," she said softly.

"OK," I said. I'd give her fucking anything.

"I want to be with you tonight. No more flirting. No more waiting."

Not what I had been expecting, but yes. That was what I wanted. "Hell, yes," I said, and pulled her up against me so I could soak her in. This was it for me.

Blaire was going to be mine after this. I would fight hell for her if I had to.

Chapter Twenty-One

Kissing had never been my thing. It was something I rarely did. But knowing how pure Blaire's mouth was and how fucking amazing she tasted made me go a little crazy when my lips touched hers. I couldn't get enough of her.

I cupped her face and devoured her. My head was screaming at me to slow down. Not to scare her or push her too fast, but God, I couldn't make my mouth listen. The Corona on her tongue as I slid mine over hers made me hungrier. The taste of beer and lime on Blaire seemed wicked. When she felt the barbell in my tongue, she pulled at the hair at the back of my head and let out a moan.

Fuck, I had to slow this down. I couldn't take her against the sink. She needed a bed and a lot of foreplay. I didn't want to hurt her. Never wanted to hurt her. I pulled away from her lips a fraction. I liked feeling her warm breath on my face. "Come with me upstairs. I want to show you my room." A grin tugged at my lips. "And my bed," I added.

She nodded, and that's all I needed. Letting go of her face, I reached for her hand. I was taking her upstairs. There were no rules where Blaire was concerned. She was on a higher plane, above any rules I had when it came to women. I just wanted her.

Pulling her by the hand in my excitement to get back to

kissing those lips of hers, I led her up the stairs. Glancing back at her as we reached the second floor, I saw the flush in her cheeks, and I broke. *Just one taste*, I told myself, then pressed her up against the nearest wall and nibbled her bottom lip before licking it and claiming her mouth again.

She melted into me easily, and I was almost sure I could make it good for her right here. I could get on my knees and kiss between her legs until she screamed my name. But no. No. We were doing this in my bed.

I tore myself away from her and took a deep breath, trying to calm myself. "One more flight of stairs," I said, more for myself than for her. Then I took her hand and led her down the hall to the door leading up to my room. I pulled the key out of my pocket. I never left my room unlocked. I liked keeping it private. Knowing no one could go in there unless I wanted them there.

The door swung open, and I stepped back and motioned for Blaire to go on in. The desire to see her in my room around my things and to share it all with her was almost as powerful as my desire to see her on my bed. Naked.

She stopped when she reached the top step and gasped. The view over the water from the floor-to-ceiling windows was what I had fallen in love with as a child.

"This room is why I had my mom buy this house. Even at ten years old, I knew this room was special," I told her, wrapping my arms around her. I loved that she could see this. That it affected her, too.

"It's incredible," she said, with awe in her voice. It *was* incredible. But having her here with me made it so much more amazing.

"I called my dad that day and told him I'd found a house I wanted to live in. He wired my mother the money, and she bought it. She loved the location, so this is the house we've spent our summers in. She has a house of her own in Atlanta, but she prefers it here."

"I'd never want to leave," she said.

Smiling, I kissed the soft skin of her ear then whispered, "Ah, but you haven't seen my cabin in Vail or my flat in Manhattan." But she would. I wanted to see her there, too.

Sharing my personal life and space with people was something I had always hated and refused to do. But with Blaire, I craved having her be a part of it. Even if all I could do was hold her, I wanted her here tonight.

I turned her toward the king-size bed that sat to the right and covered most of that far wall. "And that's my bed," I told her, as I held her hips and moved us toward the bed. I could feel Blaire tense. She was nervous. Talking about it and actually standing here in my room, looking at my bed, were two different things. I wanted her more than I wanted my next breath, but I wouldn't force her. "Blaire, even if all we do is kiss or just lie here and talk, I'm OK with that. I just wanted you up here. Close to me."

She turned back to look at me. "You don't mean that. I've seen you in action, Rush Finlay. You don't bring girls to your room and expect to just talk." Her attempt to sound teasing failed. The uncertainty in her voice sliced through me. She had come up here with me thinking she was just another one of those girls I fucked and sent home? Shit. How could I get it through to her that this thing with her was more? So much more. That she meant more.

"I don't bring girls up here at all, Blaire."

"The first night I came here, you said your bed was full," she said, frowning at me as if she had caught me in a lie. Damn, she was cute.

"Yeah, because I was sleeping in it. I don't bring girls to my bedroom. I don't want meaningless sex tainting this space. I love it here," I told her honestly. But I'd brought her here. Didn't she understand what that meant?

"The next morning, a girl was still here. You'd left her in bed, and she came looking for you in her undies," she said with a tight voice.

Crazy girl. She had no fucking idea what she did to me. Needing to touch her, I slipped my hand under her shirt and caressed the soft skin there. Her small shiver made me smile. "The first room to the right was Grant's room until our parents divorced. I use it as my bachelor-pad room now. That's where I take girls. Not here. Never here. You're my first. Well, I let Henrietta come up here once a week to clean, but I promise there is no hanky-panky going on between us," I explained, as I grinned down at her.

"Kiss me, please," she said, then grabbed my shoulders and leaned up to press her mouth against mine without waiting for me to respond.

That had to be the sweetest thing I'd ever heard. *Kiss me, please.* Fuck, this girl was gonna ruin me. I wanted her to belong to me. Her body to know only me. Completely.

Pushing her back, I laid her down on the bed and pushed her legs apart so I could settle between them without breaking the sweetest damn kiss I'd ever had. Blaire grabbed my shirt in her small fists as if she wanted to rip it off my body. If my girl wanted her hands on my chest, I'd make that a hell of a lot easier on her.

I pulled away from her long enough to jerk my shirt over my head and toss it before taking her mouth again. I could kiss her mouth for fucking hours. I had to grab handfuls of the covers to keep from stripping her naked while I let her explore. Each touch from her hands got more demanding and brave. She started out by running her hands up my arms, her touch almost as soft as a feather. But she was running them over my chest now like she couldn't get enough. When her thumbs rubbed my nipples, I swear to God I almost lost my shit.

I wanted to touch nipples, too. Her hard little pink nipples. I tore my mouth away from hers and unbuttoned the shirt she was wearing and pushed it back. I didn't have the patience to take it off. I needed her in my mouth. Now. When I jerked her bra down, both full, luscious tits fell free from their confines, and I feasted like a starving man. I licked them just to hear her moan and whimper, then I sucked hard. She bucked against me.

She hadn't been ready for that yet, and I trembled and fought to catch my breath when she cried out in pleasure from feeling my cock pressed against her needy pussy. She would be swollen and hot. I wanted to taste it. She'd tasted so sweet on my finger. I unzipped her skirt and pulled it and her panties down while keeping my eyes on her face. If she got nervous, I had to slow down. I wasn't going to frighten her. Her mouth fell open as she breathed hard and watched me. The complete trust in her eyes undid me. I wanted it all off.

I crooked my finger for her to sit up. She did so willingly, and I quickly got rid of the shirt and bra, leaving her painfully beautiful body naked. She was all mine. This was all mine. No man had touched this . . . or seen this. Fuck. Emotion overwhelmed me as I took her in. "You naked in my bed is even more unbelievably beautiful than I thought it would be . . . and trust me, I've thought about it. A lot."

Her eyes flared, and I smiled to myself. Blaire liked me to talk to her. She needed the praise. Of course she did. She was unsure of herself. This was new to her. I'd make sure she knew how ridiculously perfect she was. Leaning back over her, I pressed my throbbing erection against her now-bare pussy.

"Yes! Please!" she cried out, and scratched at my back. She was ready for me to do more. She was going to panic when she realized where I was about to put my mouth. I needed her hot and needy so she'd let me.

Lowering myself, I kissed her flat stomach and the almost bare mound, which smelled fucking amazing. Looking up at her, I held her gaze before sticking my tongue out and running my piercing directly on her very swollen clit. Blaire's scream made my cock throb as she threw her body up in an arch and grabbed the sheets in tight fists.

"God, you're sweet," I whispered against her. I was gonna get addicted to this taste. Holy fuck, it was good.

"Rush, please," she whimpered.

I stopped licking. "Please what, baby? Tell me what it is you want." She shook her head. Her eyes were closed tightly as if she were fighting to catch her breath. "I wanna hear you say it, Blaire," I told her. I wanted those naughty words coming from her mouth. I shouldn't make her, but damn, I wanted to hear it so bad.

"Please lick me again," she said with a desperate sob.

Damn, that was even better than I could have expected. I wasn't sure I would last one second once I sank into her. I started swiping my tongue through her slit with pure enjoyment. If she only knew the power she had. I'd give it all to her. She could have me on my knees and between her legs with one pout of her pretty lips. I was going to crave this.

Blaire shuddered and cried out my name while holding my head against her as if I would leave this. Once she had hit her release and no longer needed me, I reached for the condom beside my bed and ripped it open. Her eyes were starting to flutter open. I wanted to let her enjoy the high, but I couldn't. I had to get inside her. And it would ease her pain to have the nirvana of her orgasm still floating through her.

"Condom is on. I need to be inside," I whispered in her ear as I moved between her legs and ran my tip against her heat. "Holy fuck, you're so wet. It's gonna be hard not to slip right in. I'll try to go slow. I promise." I didn't want this to hurt her. Fuck, I wanted it to be good for her, because it was gonna be another level of heaven for me.

Blaire didn't tense up like I expected. Instead, she moaned and moved against me as I slowly started slipping in. Her body was clamping down on me and pulling me in like a suction. Holy hell.

"Don't move. Please, baby, don't move," I begged her. God, I couldn't hurt her, but I wanted to slam into her fully. The barrier I had been expecting met me, and I stopped. Blaire felt it and finally tensed up underneath me. "That's it. I'm gonna do it fast, but then I'll stop once I'm in and let you get used to me."

Wrapping my arms around her waist, I closed my eyes, unable to look at her. I couldn't control myself if I watched her face. Control. I needed fucking control. God, I wanted inside her completely. With one thrust, I broke through the thin wall and sank into velvet heat like I'd never known. My cock was being squeezed so damn tight I couldn't breathe. Gasping for air, I held still. She would need to adjust to me. But I wanted to move so damn bad; I wanted to fill her.

"OK, I'm OK," Blaire whispered.

Forcing my eyes open, I looked down at her. I had to be sure she wasn't just saying that. I couldn't hurt her anymore. "Are you sure? 'Cause, baby, I want to move so damn bad."

She nodded, and I watched her face as I moved back and then rocked forward inside of her.

"Does it hurt?" I asked, using every ounce of strength I had to be still and wait.

"No. I like it," she said with excitement in her eyes.

I wasn't sure I believed her, but I started to move. I had to move. My damn dick was screaming at me to move. It had never felt this kind of pleasure. Blaire moaned, and my heart slammed against my chest. Holy fuck, she was enjoying it. "You like that?" I asked.

"Yes. It feels so good."

God, yes. She was OK. I didn't have to hold back. Throwing my head back, I let out a groan of pleasure that tore from my chest as I began moving inside her. Pumping in and out of the tight suction, which pulled me in like it was fucking starving for me.

Blaire lifted her hips and grabbed my arms, meeting my thrusts. How the hell did she know to do that?

"Yeah. God, you're incredible. So tight. Blaire, you're so fucking tight." I praised her. She needed to know how amazing this was for me.

Her legs lifted and tucked close to my sides, opening her wider for me. My body sank even deeper into her warmth, and I began to tremble. I was going to come. I had reached my limit. There was only so much a man could take.

"Are you close, baby?" I asked her. I wanted her to come with me.

"I think," she said, panting as her grip on my arms tightened.

I wasn't coming without her, dammit. I wanted her to feel this with me. I moved my hand down to brush my thumb against her clit. The sensitive nub swelled under my touch.

"Ah! Yes, right there!" Blaire cried out, as her body went off underneath me.

I wasn't sure what I yelled, but a roar ripped from my chest as the most epic sensation of my life rocked through my body, sending me somewhere I didn't know existed.

Chapter Twenty-Two

Had I just blacked out? Shit. That was . . . that was . . . there were no words for what that was. I was still lying on Blaire, probably suffocating her, although her arms were tightly wrapped around my body. She wasn't trying to push me off.

I didn't want to pull out of her. Being inside her felt like home. But I had just taken her virginity and at some point lost my mind in the process.

I moved back, and she tightened her hold on me. The pleasure she gave me was more than she knew. I liked knowing she wanted me close.

"I'll be back. I need to take care of you first," I told her, then kissed her gently before getting up and heading to the bathroom.

I didn't bother with clothing. She had seen all of me now. She could handle it. I took a washcloth and got the water hot before soaking the cloth and making sure it was nice and warm. She would need cleaning up. As much as I wanted to do that again, she was going to need time.

I walked back into the room, and Blaire's eyes locked on mine then dropped to my waist. Her eyes got big, and her face turned red.

"Don't get shy on me now," I teased her. I touched her knee

and moved it. She wasn't helping. "Open up for me," I instructed, and gently nudged her knee again. "Not too much," I told her. I just needed to get better access.

The small smear of blood on her pink folds made the beast inside me roar in pleasure. This was mine. I had done this. No one had been here before me. It was fucked up, but I couldn't help it. The idea of anyone else ever touching her made me insane.

"Does it hurt?" I asked, as I cleaned the area as gently as I could. I wanted to kiss her there and make everything better, but I wasn't sure she was ready for that again just yet.

When she was as perfectly unblemished as before I had taken her, I stopped cleaning her and tossed the rag into the trash can. It was time I held her close. Let myself bask in the knowledge that she was mine. I crawled up to lie beside her and pulled her into my arms.

"I thought you weren't a cuddler, Rush," Blaire said, as she inhaled the skin on my neck with her little nose.

"I wasn't. Only with you, Blaire. You're my exception." Truer words were never spoken. Blaire was my only exception. She always would be. I tugged the covers up and over us, then tucked her head under my chin. She needed rest, and I needed to hold her. To feed the possessive beast she had awoken inside me with the reassurance that she was safe here with me.

It only took minutes before her breathing slowed and her arms went lax around me. She was exhausted. She'd worked all day . . . and then this. Smiling, I closed my eyes and inhaled her scent. The fear in the back of my head that she would leave me when she found out the truth threatened to ruin this moment. But I pushed it away. She was going to love me. I'd make her fall in love with me. Then . . . then she'd listen to me, and she'd forgive me. She had to.

I woke up to a naked, soft, beautiful body still curled up against me. The sun was peeking through the blinds. I didn't care what time it was, but I knew she would care. I wanted her here with me, but it wasn't about what I wanted. This was about Blaire. And she wouldn't want to be late for work. Her sense of responsibility wouldn't allow that. I had to wake her up, as much as letting her sleep in my arms appealed to me.

Taking a deep breath, I let her scent fill my head. The memory of her other scent made my already semierect cock go full-blown. I wasn't going to make her do something that would be painful, but I could make her tender flesh feel good and ease my hunger.

I moved down her body and picked up one of her adorable bare feet, then placed a kiss to the instep. She didn't move. Grinning, I continued trailing kisses up to her calf and back down again, tasting her skin every few kisses.

Blaire's body started to stretch and move. Just a little at first, but the moment she was awake, I knew it. The slow, easy movements stopped, and her eyes flew open. I continued kissing up her leg, grinning while I watched her sleepy face.

"There's your eyes. I was beginning to wonder just how much I was going to need to kiss in order to wake you up. Not that I mind kissing higher, but that would lead to some more incredible sex, and you now only have twenty minutes to get to work."

Blaire's eyes went wide, and she sat up in bed so quickly I had to let her leg go. I knew she wouldn't want to miss work.

"You've got time. I'll go fix you something to eat while you get ready," I said. I wanted to spend breakfast between her legs, but again, it wasn't about Rush's wants at that moment.

"Thank you, but you don't have to. I'll grab something in the break room when I get there," she said, blushing as she grabbed the sheet to keep her bare breasts covered. The affectionate woman from last night was gone, and a nervous, unsure one was in her place. What had I done wrong?

"I want you to eat here. Please," I said, watching her closely.

The small flare in her eyes told me she needed to hear that. Did she need reassurance? "OK," she said. "I need to go to my room and get a shower." She still looked nervous.

I wanted her to stay up here. I wanted her using my things. But . . . fuck. "I'm torn, because I want you to shower in there, but I don't think I'll be able to walk away knowing you're naked and soapy in my shower. I'll want to join you," I admitted.

"As appealing as that sounds, I'd be late for work," she said with a small smile.

"Right. You need to go to your room." She looked around for her discarded clothes. I wanted her in my clothes this morning. When she walked out of my room looking like a rumpled angel, I wanted my shirt against her skin, covering up what belonged to me. "Put this on. Henrietta comes today. I'll have her wash and press your clothes from last night," I said, picking up the shirt I had worn last night and tossing it to her.

She didn't argue. I couldn't look away while she pulled my shirt over her head and let the sheet fall once she was sure I couldn't see her tits. Guess the fact that I'd sucked on them and lapped at them like a man obsessed last night didn't matter. She was covering up this morning.

"Now, stand up. I want to see you," I told her, needing to see her in my shirt. It was an image I intended to burn into my brain for eternity.

She stood up, and the shirt hit her thighs. Knowing how naked she was underneath and how easily I could pick her up and spread her legs had me rethinking my plans for today.

"Can you call in sick?" I asked, looking up at her hopefully.

"I'm not sick," she replied, with a frown between her brows.

"Are you sure? Because I think I have a fever," I said playfully, stepping around the bed and pulling her into my arms. "Last night was amazing." I pressed my nose into her hair.

Her arms came around my waist and held tightly. "I have to work today. They're expecting me."

That was Blaire. It was one of the many things that had attracted me to her. She wasn't going to lie or ignore a responsibility. Letting her go, I stepped back and put distance between us. "I know. Run, Blaire. Run your cute little ass downstairs and get ready. I can't promise you I will let you go if you stand here looking like that much longer."

A grin broke out across her face, and she took off running for the stairs. Her laughter trailed behind her, and all I could do was stand there like a fool and smile.

I got showered and dressed quickly, then called Jace. I didn't want to ask Blaire about her schedule, but I wanted an excuse to be at the club. I never went up there unless Nan wanted me to meet her for golf or dinner.

"Hello?" Jace said, sounding surprised that I was calling.

"Hey. Are y'all golfing today?" I asked.

"Uh, yeah. We golf every day. You know that."

"I want in," I said.

"You're gonna golf?" he asked, shock in his voice.

I didn't see what the big deal was. I had golfed with them before. I played with Nan and Grant on occasion. "Yeah, so?" I said.

Jace chuckled. "OK, sure. You haven't played with us in forever. What gives today? Normally, you have to be dragged out onto the course by Nan or Grant."

I wasn't answering that. He didn't need to get the wrong idea about Blaire. They would need to see me with her. I'd make sure they all knew how off-limits she was. "In the mood for golf," I replied.

"All right, then. See you at eleven thirty. Woods has to be in a meeting this afternoon with his dad, so we're playing early."

I didn't point out that most people thought an early tee time was six or seven in the morning. Not eleven thirty. "Thanks. See you then."

I headed downstairs to see if Blaire had left yet. She couldn't have had time to dress and eat. Not if she took a shower. I opened the door at the bottom of my stairs and looked to the right. Blaire's door was open. She wasn't in there. The lights were off.

I headed for the stairs and took them two at a time, hoping to catch her in time for a good-bye kiss. She was standing at the bar, with a bowl of cereal in her hands and a spoon lifted to her mouth. She was eating. Good.

"Don't let me stop you," I said, walking over to the coffee pot, not wanting to make her nervous. She seemed so jumpy. "Are you working inside today?" I asked. She shook her head no then swallowed.

"They need me outside today," she said.

I turned back to the coffee pot before smiling. I would see her, then. I fucking loved golf. I noticed her cell phone lying on the counter and picked it up. She had forgotten it already.

I switched the pot on and watched her walk to the sink with her bowl. I stepped over and blocked her path and took the bowl from her, setting it in the sink behind me.

"Are you . . . is everything OK?" I asked, then slipped my hand down to gently cup the place between her legs, which I worried would bother her today. She had to work outside in the heat, and I didn't want it to be painful.

She blushed and ducked her head. "I'm fine," she said in a breathy voice.

"If you were staying here, I'd make it feel better," I told her.

Her breathing quickened. "I can't. I have to go to work," she said, lifting her eyes to meet mine.

I slipped her phone into the pocket of her shorts. I wanted it on her all the time. "I can't stand the idea of you hurting and me not being able to do anything about it," I told her, slowly caressing the outside of her shorts.

"I have to hurry. I had to skip the shower, which is terrible, I know, but I couldn't shower and eat. I didn't want you . . . I wanted to eat so you would be happy," she said.

She hadn't showered. Well, fuck. I buried my head in the curve of her neck and inhaled deeply. "Shit, Blaire. I love that you're gonna smell like me all damn day," I admitted. Knowing that she hadn't washed me off made my inner beast roar. I was getting out of hand.

"I gotta go," she said, stepping back. With a small wave, she hurried for the door.

It wasn't until I heard the door close that I realized I hadn't gotten my kiss. She'd distracted me with the fact that she was still wearing me all over her body. The stupid grin on my face was starting to make my face hurt. I hadn't smiled this much in a lifetime, yet that girl kept giving me a reason to.

Chapter Twenty-Three

Back on the cart today? As much as I like having you inside, this makes golfing a hell of a lot more fun," Woods said to Blaire when she'd pulled the cart up beside the first hole.

I was going to set that shit straight right fucking now. "Back off, Woods. That's a little too close," I warned, as I walked toward them. Blaire spun around with a surprised look on her face. She hadn't been expecting me. She would soon find out she couldn't get rid of me.

"So she's why you suddenly wanted to play with us today?" Woods asked, sounding annoyed.

I wasn't interested in answering him. My focus was on Blaire. Her hairline was wet from sweat already. It was hot out here today, and she could be suffering. If she was hurting at all, then Woods was going to let her go home. I'd throw her over my shoulder and leave with her if I needed to. I slid my hand around her waist and tugged her against me possessively before lowering my head so I could whisper in her ear. "Are you sore?" I asked her.

"I'm fine," she replied.

I kissed her ear, but I wasn't ready to let her go yet. "Do you feel stretched? Can you tell I've been inside you?" I asked.

As much as I didn't want her hurting, I wanted her to feel me there. To remember I had been there.

She nodded and melted against me. Little Blaire liked me talking naughty. I would need to remember that.

"Good. I like knowing you can feel where I've been," I said, then leveled my gaze at Woods. I wanted to make sure he understood me.

"I figured this was gonna happen," Woods said, sounding pissed.

"Nan know it yet?" Jace asked, and Thad, one of Woods and Jace's close friends, nudged him as if to shut him up.

"This isn't Nan's business. Or yours," I replied, glaring at Jace. He needed to listen to Thad and shut up. I would deal with Nan. They didn't know shit.

"I came here to golf. Let's not talk about this out here. Blaire, why don't you get everyone's drinks and head on to the next hole?" Woods said.

I didn't like him bossing her around. He was doing it on purpose. The fucker had better watch himself. His daddy would have me in his office real damn quick. Finlay money kept this place going.

I wouldn't do this in front of Blaire, because it would upset her, but Woods was going to be set straight.

Blaire stepped out of my arms and went to get everyone's drinks. She handed me a Corona without asking what I wanted. She handed Woods his beer, and he slipped a fucking hundred-dollar bill into her hands. I could see the way her shoulders tensed as she cut her eyes toward me and quickly stuck it in her pocket. I would not get pissed because he paid her well. He could afford it, and she deserved it for working for his sorry ass. Bastard.

I walked over to her and placed two hundred-dollar bills in her pocket, then pressed a kiss to her lips. I was staking my claim, and they'd all better fucking get that. I winked at her and headed over to the caddy. I wouldn't look at Woods until Blaire was gone, because one smirk from him, and I would break his goddamn nose.

When I glanced back, I saw Blaire driving away. I pulled out my phone and sent her a text.

I'm sorry about Woods.

He had been an ass, and I was worried that she was upset. He was her boss. She needed to know he wouldn't do that again.

I'm fine. Woods is my boss. No big deal.

Was she used to him acting like this? Yeah, he and I were gonna talk. Now.

"So, you and Blaire, huh? Didn't see that coming," Jace said, grinning like an idiot.

Woods let out a bitter laugh.

I stepped over to stand in front of him. "Do you want to say something to me, Woods? Because if you do, go ahead and say it now, because I sure as shit got something to say to you."

The anger in Woods's eyes didn't surprise me. He didn't like being reminded that he couldn't intimidate me. He shook his head at me and looked out to where Blaire's cart had disappeared over the hill. "She's too good for you to fuck with. I thought there was some chance you'd have enough heart not to touch her. She deserves so much more than she's gonna get from you. If she had so much as given me a chance, I would have shown her how she deserved to be treated. But you." He pointed at my chest. "You, Finlay, you just crook your son-of-a-rock-star finger, and they come running to you. And you toss them away without a thought. Blaire isn't worldly enough to handle that. She's not that tough, damn you." He looked like he would slam his fist into my face.

The only reason I let him stand there and yell at me was that he didn't understand. He thought I was using her. He wanted to protect her. He wasn't gonna get to, because I wasn't letting him near her, but I appreciated the fact that he saw what I did. Blaire was precious. I shoved him back enough to get him out of my face. "Do you actually think I would have touched her had I not known all that? You think I would have threatened my sister for just anyone? No. Blaire isn't just another girl for me. She's it for me. She. Is. It."

Saying the words out loud didn't just shock everyone around me, it shocked the hell out of me, too. She was it.

I would never want anyone else.

Ever.

Just Blaire.

"Motherfucker," Jace whispered from behind me. "Rush Finlay did not just say what I think he said."

Woods's angry glare slowly dissipated. As my words sank into his thick skull, I saw disbelief and then acceptance cross his face. "Shit," he finally said.

I stepped back and shrugged. "You said it yourself. Except you were wrong about one thing. She isn't special. She's fucking perfect." I turned around, then stopped and looked back at him pointedly. "And she's mine," I said, loudly enough for all of them to hear me. Swinging my eyes in a warning glare to the other two, who were watching me as if I had lost my mind, I repeated, "Mine. Blaire is mine."

"Well, shiiit," Thad finally said. "Guess I shoulda paid more attention to the new girl. She's got the biggest player I know tied up in knots. Day-um, I'm impressed."

This time, Jace shoved Thad. "Shut up," he hissed.

"Let's play some golf," I said, taking my driver and heading for the tee.

I had a late lunch with Grant and then headed home to shower and decide what to do with Blaire tonight. Although sex was pretty damn high on my priority list, I knew she needed to take it easy. I also wanted to talk. There was so much I didn't know about her. I wanted to know everything. I wanted to sit and listen to her talk to me. Tell me things.

Taking her out was an option, but I was greedy. I didn't want to share her yet. I wanted all her attention. I didn't want to know that others were getting to look at her. I just wanted it to be us here in this house alone. Together.

Then, of course, I wanted to kiss her all over her body and taste the sweetness between her legs again. But first, I wanted to talk. I didn't want this to be a sexual thing only. For the first time in my life, I wanted to let someone in. I didn't want to keep Blaire out. She needed to love me. For me to survive this, she would have to love me. How the hell I would get her to fall in love with me I didn't know. Getting to know her would help. Eating her pussy wasn't the way to her heart. I had to remind myself that my addiction to tasting her couldn't take over. Did I love her? I hadn't ever been in love. Other than my dad, Nan, and Grant, I couldn't say I had ever loved anyone else.

Would I choose her over one of them?

Yes.

Would I die to protect her?

Hell, yes.

Could I live if she left me?

No. I would be shattered.

Was this love? It seemed so much stronger than something as simple as love.

A knock on my bedroom door broke into my thoughts. Shit. It wasn't Grant. Nan was here. Not who I wanted to deal with right now. I took my time going to the door. Her banging just got louder.

Jerking the door open, I was greeted by my sister's tear-streaked face. She wasn't allowed in my room. I hadn't actually told her that, but it was understood. I stepped into the hallway and closed the door behind me.

Nan was pointing at the room Blaire was sleeping in . . . or, rather, keeping her things in. She would be sleeping with me from now on.

"So it's true! She's in there. You let her move up here? Are you fucking her, too? Is that what this is? She's not that attractive, Rush. It isn't like you can't have anyone you want. She's just another pretty face. Why can't you not fuck her? Do you have no control over your damn dick? She can't be that good in bed!"

"Stop!" I roared before she said any more. Nan was pushing me. I hated that she had been crying, but with Nan, you never knew if those were real tears or not. I hadn't seen her actually crying, so I couldn't be sure. But I didn't want her upset. I just wanted her to let me be happy. For once in my goddamn life to let me make a decision for myself. Not for her.

"Don't yell at me!" Real tears filled her eyes as she started crying again. OK, so maybe she really was upset. I didn't yell at her often. She didn't normally piss me off so bad. "Since . . ." She sniffed. "Since she got here, you've been yelling at me. All the time. I can't . . ." She let out another sob. "I can't stand this. You've turned on me. For her."

This wasn't Blaire's fault. Why couldn't Nan see that? This was like talking in circles. I reached out and pulled her into my arms. The little girl I had taken care of my entire life was looking at me through swollen eyes. I was all she had. "I'm sorry for yelling at you," I told her, and she sobbed harder against my chest.

"I just . . . just . . . don't understand," she said.

Telling Nan that I was in love with Blaire wasn't the answer to this. For starters, I hadn't told Blaire I loved her, and I needed to tell her first. Second, Nan would lose her shit if I told her that. She could go from pitiful, sobbing mess to wild, insane tornado in a second. I had witnessed that more than once. "It isn't about the sex. I've tried to tell you that Blaire isn't to blame. I've tried explaining to you how she's been wronged here, too. You aren't the only victim. You shouldn't hate someone who has suffered the way you have. I don't understand why you can't see that, Nan. I love you. I will always love you. You know that. But I can't choose you over her. Not this time. This time, you're asking for too much. I won't give her up."

Nan stilled in my arms. I wanted to hope that she was listening to me, that I was getting through to her, but I knew my sister. That would be too damn easy. It would take something much bigger to get her to give up a hatred she had held on to most of her life. "Why can't you give her money and send her away?" Nan asked quietly, as she leaned back from my embrace and crossed her arms over her chest defensively.

"Because I can't let her go. She . . . she makes me happy, Nan." I admitted that much to her.

Nan's eyes flashed the anger I knew would ignite if she thought for a minute that I felt more for Blaire than I did for her. As fucked up as that was, Nan expected to be my number one her entire life. She never considered what would happen if I fell in love one day. She was so desperate to be someone's number one that she was determined to force it on me. "Because she's a good fuck?" she said sourly.

I closed my eyes tightly and took a deep breath. Keeping my calm was important. Losing it with Nan again wouldn't help anything. When I opened my eyes, I leveled my gaze on my sister. "Nan. Don't do that again. Blaire is not a fuck for me. Get that through your head. She isn't controlling me with sex. She's more than that."

Nan stiffened and turned her head to glare at the open door to Blaire's room. "You don't even know her. You just met her. Yet you want to choose her over me," she spat.

"I do know her. I've been sharing a home with her for weeks now. I've been unable to keep my eyes off her. I've watched her. I've talked to her. I know her. She's . . . God, Nan, she's what makes me happy. Can't you accept that? Let this thing with her go!"

Nan didn't look at me or respond. The fight was done for now, but I knew I hadn't won. She wasn't over this.

We stood in silence for a few moments, and I waited for her to say something. Whatever she was deciding needed to be dealt with carefully. Nan held the power to ruin things for me. She could tell Blaire everything, and I'd lose. I couldn't lose Blaire.

"I want to have friends over here tonight," she said, swinging her gaze back to me.

Fine. She was going to force one of her parties on me. Typical Nan. She needed to know that I would still give in to her on some level. "OK," I replied without argument. I would take Blaire up to my room, and we would be away from the crowd and noise.

Nan nodded, then turned and walked away. That was it. For now.

Chapter Twenty-Four

I wasn't in the mood for this, but I'd told Nan she could have her party. I should have expected she'd overdo it without me giving her any guidelines. I wasn't drinking tonight. I intended to spend my night with Blaire. The guys may have been informed of the fact that Blaire was off-limits, but the females hadn't accepted that I wasn't available. I shook my head at another of Nan's friends who was offering to give me a blow job right in front of everyone.

Grant's eyes met mine over the crowd. He was kicked back on the sofa, with a girl I had said no to earlier half-sitting in his lap. He rolled his eyes and took a swig of his beer. I had asked him to come and monitor things tonight. I didn't want interruptions. He had agreed, as long as he could stay in his usual room if one of the females piqued his interest.

I didn't care what he did, as long as no one bothered Blaire and me. I nodded my head in the direction of the girl I had just sent away. If he wanted easy, adventurous sex, I was sure that one was a good choice.

He raised his eyebrows in interest and watched her saunter into the living room. I was going to head upstairs and wait for Blaire in her room. She shouldn't be too much longer now.

"You going up?" Nan asked.

I nodded. "Yeah. Grant's here if you need him."

"What about her? Is she gonna stay up there, too?" Nan asked, trying to look like she didn't care what Blaire did.

"Blaire will be with me. Good night, Nan. Enjoy your party."

She spun on her heels and stalked toward the kitchen. I turned to look back at Grant, and he just shook his head. He knew Nan was giving me shit about Blaire. I could tell he wasn't on board with the not-telling-Blaire idea. He thought I should tell her now before it went too far.

Problem with that was that I had already let it go too far.

Blaire's room smelled like her already. I didn't turn on the lights. I could see the moonlight on the Gulf better in the darkness. Sitting down on the end of her bed, I inhaled, trying to feed my hunger for her. She would be here any minute. But I was growing impatient. If I could get her to stop working and let me take care of her, I would, but I knew better than to suggest that. Blaire would throw a fit. I'd had to lie to her to get her to take the damn cell phone. She was still planning to pay me for the food in my kitchen. I was just going to find a way to put that back in her savings. Somehow. Stubborn woman wouldn't take anything from me but my body. I grinned at that thought. I was more than willing to give her my body. She would also gladly accept my tongue. She had a thing for my tongue. The way her eyes danced with anticipation when she saw my piercing was so damn sexy.

I heard footsteps and turned to see Blaire enter the room. Both her hands flew to her mouth to cover a startled scream, which died the moment she realized it was me. I stood up and walked toward her. I couldn't not touch her a moment longer.

"Hey," I said.

"Hey," she replied, and then a frown tugged on her lips. "What are you doing in here?"

Where else would I be? "Waiting for you. I kinda thought that was obvious."

She ducked her head to hide the pleased smile I still saw on her lips. "I can see that. But you have guests," she said.

I had already forgotten they were here. My focus had been completely on her. "Not my guests. Trust me, I wanted an empty house," I assured her, and cupped the side of her face. "Come upstairs with me. Please."

She tossed her purse onto the bed, then slipped her hand into mine. "Lead the way."

I managed to let her get to the top step before pulling her into my arms and pressing my lips to hers. All day, I had thought about how good she tasted and how I loved the feel of her tongue sliding against mine.

She wrapped her arms around my neck, kissing me back eagerly. The longing in her kiss matched mine, and I knew I had to stop now if I intended to have a talk with her tonight.

I tore myself away from her. "Talk. We are going to talk first. I want to see you smile and laugh. I want to know what your favorite show was when you were a kid and who made you cry at school and what boy band you hung posters of on your wall. Then I want you naked in my bed again," I said.

She smiled and walked over to the sofa. Images of her

naked on my large sectional flashed in my head, and I had to shake it to stop myself. *Not the plan, Rush.*

"Thirsty?" I asked, opening the fridge I kept in my room.

"Just some ice water would be nice."

I started fixing her a glass of ice water and thinking about everything I wanted to know. Not how she looked when she came.

"*Rugrats* was my favorite show. Ken Norris made me cry at least once a week, but then he'd make Valerie cry, and I'd get mad and hurt him. My favorite and most successful attack was a swift kick to the balls. And, I'm ashamed to admit, the Backstreet Boys covered my walls." Blaire had answered every question I had mentioned.

I handed her the water and sat beside her on the sofa. "Who's Valerie?" I asked. She had never mentioned her friends. I assumed she didn't have many because of her mom.

Blaire tensed up beside me, and my interest further intensified. Had Valerie hurt her? "Valerie was my twin sister. She died in a car accident four years ago. My dad was driving. A year later, he walked out of our lives and never returned. Mom said we had to forgive him, because he couldn't live with the fact that he'd been driving the car that killed Valerie. I always wanted to believe her. Even when he didn't come to Mom's funeral, I wanted to believe he just couldn't face it. So I forgave him. I didn't hate him or let bitterness and hate control me. But I came here, and . . . well, you know. I guess Mom was wrong."

Shit. Holy shit. My stomach felt sick. I leaned back on the sofa and put my arm around her. I wanted to pull her into my lap and console her. Tell her I'd do anything she asked to make this better. To fix this. To change the past, I would move heaven and hell. But I couldn't do that. So I said all I could say. "I had no idea you had a twin sister." That was a lie. I had known. But it was so easy to forget that the girl I knew these facts about was the same woman I was completely in love with. The one who suffered from what I had done.

"We were identical. You couldn't tell us apart. We had a lot of fun with that at school and with boys. Only Cain could tell us apart."

I slipped my hand into her hair and played with the silky strands. "How long did your parents know each other before they married?" I asked. I wanted to hear it from her. There was so much truth I was afraid I didn't know. So many lies I had believed.

"It was a love-at-first-sight kind of thing. Mom was visiting a friend of hers in Atlanta. Dad had recently broken up with her friend, and he came around one night when Mom was at her friend's apartment alone. Her friend was a little wild, from what my mom said. Dad took one look at Mom, and he was sunk. I can't blame him. My mom was gorgeous. She had my color hair, but she had the biggest green eyes. They were like jewels, almost, and she was fun. You were happy just to be near her. Nothing ever got her down. She smiled through everything. The only time I saw her cry was when she was told about Valerie. She crumpled to the floor and wailed that day. It would have frightened me if I hadn't felt the same way. It was like part of my soul had been ripped out." Blaire stopped, and I felt her quick intake of breath. I couldn't imagine losing Nan or Grant. Yet she'd lost her twin. Then her father. Then her mother. My chest constricted in pain.

I held her against me. "I'm so sorry, Blaire. I had no idea."

Blaire turned her head up and pressed her lips to mine hungrily.

She was seeking comfort, and this was the only way she knew how to get it from me. I wanted her to know that she could climb into my arms, and that I'd hold her tight whenever she needed me. But I couldn't say that right now. Not yet.

"I love them. I will always love them, but I'm OK now. They're together. They have each other," she said, pulling back from the kiss. She was trying to make me feel better. She had lost them, and she was trying to comfort me about it.

"Who do you have?" I asked, feeling more emotion than I'd ever felt in my life.

"I have me. I found out three years ago, when my mom got sick, that as long as I held on to me and didn't forget who I was, I'd always be OK," she said with determination.

I couldn't breathe. Fuck that. I didn't deserve to breathe.

She was so damn strong. She had faced hell, and she was still finding reasons to smile. She didn't think she needed anyone. But God, I needed her. I wasn't as strong as she was. I didn't deserve her. But I wasn't a good guy. I would never do the right thing and stop this, because I wouldn't be able to physically watch her walk away. Panic and desperation settled in my chest.

"I need you. Right now. Let me love you right here, please," I begged her. I was ready to plead. This wasn't right. She needed someone to listen to her and hold her, but here I was begging her to take care of me.

Blaire pulled her shirt off and reached for mine. I lifted my arms and let her take it off me. I liked having her undress me. Reaching behind her, I unsnapped her bra and threw it aside. Cupping her full breasts in my hands, I let their heaviness fill my palms.

"You are so fucking unbelievably gorgeous. Inside and out," I told her. "As much as I don't deserve it, I want to be buried inside you. I can't wait. I just need to get as close to you as I can get."

Blaire moved away from me, causing her breasts to sway and bounce. My mouth watered, and my palms itched to reach out and squeeze them. Fondle their perfect satin plumpness in my hands again. Then she started taking off her shoes. My eyes fell to her hands, which were now working on the button on her shorts. She was stripping for me. No bashfulness about her body like this morning. I wasn't going to have to coax her clothes off again.

She shimmied and stepped out of her shorts, and I was pretty sure I was panting loudly.

"Get naked," she demanded, and her gaze dropped to my obvious arousal.

Holy shit. Where had my sweet Blaire gone? I didn't argue. I stood and discarded my jeans, then reached for her and pulled her toward me as I sat back down. "Straddle me," I told her.

She did as instructed. Her thighs were open, and the sweetness of her heat met my nose. I wanted to taste her. But that would have to wait.

"Now," I managed to say through the emotion in my voice. "Ease down on me."

I grabbed my cock and held it so she could sink down on

me. I wasn't sure if this was a good position for just her second time, but I wanted to try. She held on to my shoulders with both hands.

"Easy, baby. Slow and easy. You're gonna be sore."

She nodded just as my tip brushed against her opening. I moved it over her slit, causing her to tremble as I brushed her clit with it.

"That's it. You're getting so fucking wet. God, I want to taste it." I knew she liked me to tell her what I was thinking. I loved being able to talk dirty to her and not scare her.

Her gaze locked with mine, and she shifted until I was brushing her entrance. Her small, perfect white teeth came out and bit down on her bottom lip, and then she sank down on me hard and fast. Her cry echoed through the room, and I removed my hand, letting her take me completely.

"Shit!" I groaned as her heat squeezed me tightly with that insane suction that had driven me mad last night. Somehow it was more intense tonight. She was hotter, and *holy fuck*, she was wet. Like slick velvet encasing me until she killed me from the pleasure.

I had started to ask if she was OK when her mouth covered mine and her tongue tangled wildly with mine. Her taste. Oh, God, her taste was so good. I cupped her face with my hands and devoured her mouth. Both my tongue and my dick were buried inside Blaire's sweet body, and I fought to keep from grabbing her and fucking her like a maniac. She threw her head back and grabbed my shoulders tighter, then began riding me like she couldn't get enough. The fear that she was in pain vanished when I took in the look of pure bliss on her face as she rode me hard and fast. My gaze dropped to her tits, bouncing with each time she lifted and slammed back down onto my cock.

"Blaire, oh, holy fuck, Blaire," I growled, unable to believe this.

My hands grabbed her waist, and I lost my mind. I wanted to cherish her, but damn, I wanted to fuck her, too. I wanted to fuck her body with complete abandon. It was the most exciting, mind-blowing thing I'd ever experienced.

"Shit, baby. GOD, Blaire. Yeah, that's it baby girl, fuck me." The words were pouring out of my mouth and I couldn't stop myself. "Your tight pussy is fucking perfect. Sucking my dick, *shit*, no pussy should feel this good. Holy hell, baby. That's it. Fuck me. Fuck me, Blaire. Sweetest fucking pussy in the world." Then it hit me. I had never fucked without a condom before. Holy fuck, I wasn't wearing a condom. I was clean. I had been checked recently. I never went without a condom, but . . . she squeezed me, and I couldn't make myself care. God, I wanted this with her. Nothing between us.

Blaire's movements changed, and she began rocking back and forth. My mouth greedily searched for her nipples and sucked at them as they bounced in front of me. "I'm gonna come," she moaned, rocking harder.

"Fuck, baby, so good."

And then she was screaming my name, jerking against me as her body shuddered. I exploded inside her, wrapping my arms around her waist to keep from falling off the fucking earth without her. Her name fell from my lips more than once. My body vibrated and trembled as I fought to breathe. My release shot inside her, marking her. The beast inside me roared to life. *Mine. Mine. Mine.*

Blaire's sex was still clenching me tightly as spasms hit her body. Each time she clamped down on my cock, I cried out. It was like I was coming again over and over. There wasn't an end to this.

Finally, her body began to relax, releasing my dick from the clamp of pure nirvana it had been pulled into. Her arms wrapped around my neck, and she fell into me, completely spent.

"Never. Never in all my life," I managed to gasp through the lack of oxygen. "That was . . . God, Blaire, I don't have words." I couldn't stop touching her. Stroking her back and cupping her ass in my hands, I let my body enjoy the aftermath.

"I believe the word you are looking for is *epic*," Blaire said. Laughter bubbled up from her chest, and she leaned back to look at me.

"The most epic sex ever known to man," I assured her. "I'm ruined. You know that, right? You've ruined me."

She wiggled on my lap. I was still buried inside her. I wasn't ready to move just yet. The fact that my cock could even stir again this soon after sex surprised me. "Hmmm, no, I think you might still work," she said, grinning wickedly.

"God, woman, you're gonna have me hard and ready again. I need to clean you up," I told her.

She stared at me with an emotion I was too scared to hope for, then traced my bottom lip with the tip of her finger. "I won't bleed again. I did that already," she said shyly.

I pulled her finger into my mouth and sucked on it. I knew I had to tell her. She hadn't realized the impact of having sex without a condom yet. I didn't want to ruin this moment, but she had to know I didn't have anything that could harm her.

And if she wasn't on birth control, it was still very unlikely that we had just made a baby. It took most couples months of trying. One mishap wouldn't do it. "I wasn't wearing a condom. I'm clean, though. I always wear a condom, and I get checked regularly," I told her calmly.

She didn't move or speak.

Shit. "I'm sorry. You got naked, and my brain kind of checked out. I promise you I'm clean," I assured her.

"No, it's OK. I believe you. I didn't think about it, either," she said, the shock still on her face.

I pulled her back against me. "Good, because that was fucking unbelievable. I've never felt it without a condom. Knowing I was in you and feeling you bare makes me real damn happy. You felt amazing. All hot and wet and so very tight."

She rocked against me, and my cock started growing again. God, she felt good. "Mmm," she murmured.

I wanted more. Like this. Just here. But . . . "Are you on any birth control?"

She shook her head. Of course she wasn't. She had no reason to be. We were going to have to change that, though. I would have to have her bare again. Now that I knew how she felt, there was no going back.

Groaning, I moved her until I was no longer buried inside her. "We can't do that again until you are. But you've got me all hard again." I reached down and ran my finger over her swollen clit. She was already turned on again, too. "So sexy," I whispered, as I watched the small bud pulse against my thumb. She threw her head back and moaned. I needed to have her again. I would pull out this time. I just . . . oh, fuck, I had to be inside her. "Blaire, come take a shower with me," I said.

"OK."

She let me guide her to the bathroom. I turned on the heated floors when we walked in so that the marble floor wouldn't be so cold to her bare feet. Then I turned on the shower heads and the steamer option. Turning back, I took her hand. "I want you in the shower. What we did out there was the best fuck I've ever had in my life. But in here, it's gonna be slower. I'll take care of you." I pulled her into the large shower. Water hit us from directly overhead and from the two shower heads mounted on each side wall. Closing the door, I pressed the sealer so that the steam would fill the shower.

Blaire was looking around with awe. "I didn't know they made showers this big or this complicated. You have water coming from everywhere—and is that steam?"

Grinning, I pulled her over toward the large bench. "Hold on to my shoulders," I told her, before reaching down, taking her leg, and lifting it until her foot was on the bench. Her pussy was completely open to me, and I didn't say anything more. I filled my hands with body wash and worked it into a lather before moving to wash the insides of her thighs.

"Rush!" She gasped, squeezing my shoulders and leaning into me more.

I continued washing my come off her thighs, where it had leaked out of her, making them sticky. Lifting my head, I watched her face as I touched her tender folds. I didn't want to burn or sting her, I just wanted to clean her.

Her eyelids fluttered closed, and she moaned and rocked against my hand. I'd wanted to wash her first, before I sank back into her again, but if she kept this up, I wasn't going to be able to stop myself.

"Feel good?" I asked her. She only nodded. Her eyes closed, and her head tilted slightly back. The water had soaked her hair, and it was slicked back off her face. I trailed kisses across her forehead and down her cheeks as I continued to wash her. "Is it sore?" I asked against her ear.

She shivered. "Yes. But I like being sore. Knowing that you made me sore from . . ." She paused. "Fucking me," she finished in a whisper.

"Blaire, baby, I'm gonna have to fuck you now. You shouldn't have said that dirty word. I can't keep being good and making you feel better." The edge in my voice gave away how close I was to grabbing her and bending her over.

She opened her eyes, and the heat in her gaze burned me. "Will you fuck me against the wall?" she asked, her breathing heavy.

"Any way you want, sweet Blaire."

I cupped my hands and filled them with water, which I used to clean the soap between her legs. When I had it all off, I grabbed her and shoved her against the wall. But I caught myself. I was doing it sweet and easy now. She might say she liked it, but tomorrow she would be tender, and I had to remember to be gentle.

"I'm not using a condom. I can't. I need to feel you. But I swear I'll pull out before I come," I told her.

"OK. Just please, Rush, put it in," she begged.

My control snapped.

Chapter Twenty-Five

Opening my eyes against the bright sunlight, I squinted, realizing I had forgotten to close the blinds last night. Then Blaire's scent hit me, and I rolled over to an empty bed. Shit. She was gone.

I had slept through her leaving for work. Dammit. I had wanted to kiss her good morning. Did she remember to eat breakfast? Frustrated, I threw the covers off and sat up. Blaire had a job. I had to accept that. She wouldn't let me not accept it. Even if it sucked. I didn't like her working so much, especially after I had kept her busy most of the night. There had been very little sleep.

She was going to be so tired today. When she got off work, I would feed her and then give her a massage and bathe her. Tonight I would make up for the fact that I had fucked her like a madman all night. We would go to bed early. She would get her rest. I could keep from fucking her for one night. But I would probably eat her pussy. I only had so much self-restraint.

I decided to skip a shower. I could smell Blaire on my skin, and I wasn't willing to wash that off just yet. I wanted to be reminded for the rest of the day of how fucking lucky I was.

By the time I had made my way downstairs to get something to eat, it was almost noon. The doorbell chimed, and urgent knocking followed. "Rush! Open the door! My hands are full!" Nan yelled from the other side.

Crap.

I opened the door, and my sister stood there with her hair up in large rollers, several shopping bags, and a garment bag that said "Marc Jacobs." What the hell?

"Nan, why are you at my door with shopping bags? And last time I checked, there wasn't a Marc Jacobs or"—I glanced at the bags in her hands—"Burberry or Chanel or Saks in Rosemary Beach. Where did this shit come from?"

Nan dropped her bags and looked at me like I was the one who had lost my mind. "Manhattan. I bought them when I was there last month. I have two dresses from Marc Jacobs that I'm just not sure about. And then the shoes . . . that's another story. I can't even begin to decide. I need to know what you plan on wearing, and I need to use the bathroom in Mom's room for my stylist to fix my hair and makeup. There's more room here than at my place. Besides, this way, we can ride together," she said, as if any of what she was saying made sense.

I had no idea what the hell she thought I was doing, but if a naked Blaire wasn't involved, neither was I. "What are you talking about?" I asked, wishing I had gotten at least one cup of coffee before Nan had arrived with her crazy ranting.

She froze halfway up the stairs and turned to look at me. Her face said drama was about to ensue. Shit. "Tonight, Rush. Did you forget? Really?" Nan's voice went an octave higher, and I knew she was about to get hysterical.

Fuck, I needed some coffee.

"Oh, my God! You did forget. You're so wrapped up in *her*

that you can't remember something this important to *me*." Nan was now yelling.

I closed my eyes and rubbed my temples, hoping I wouldn't end up with a headache from this. I just wanted to drink coffee and plan my evening with Blaire. Not this mess. "Nan, I just woke up. Please stop yelling at me," I said.

"Stop yelling? You're really going to tell me to stop yelling when my own brother forgot that tonight is the debutante ball? I've been planning my debutante ball since I was five. You know that. You know how important tonight is. But you *forgot*!"

Motherfucker. I did not want to escort my sister to a ball where a bunch of spoiled females dressed up and tried to outdo one another for hours. Blaire did not factor into this equation, and I wanted to be with Blaire.

"You don't want to go," Nan said with a loud wail. She sounded like a child.

"I forgot. I'm sorry. But you haven't mentioned it in months, and you know this isn't my thing."

Nan threw down the bag in her hand.

Great. We were going to have a temper tantrum with articles of clothing that cost me a fucking fortune. Blaire was working her ass off daily, and my sister was buying shoes with my money that cost more than Blaire could make in two weeks. Fucking unfair. I hated this. I hated not being able to give Blaire everything she wanted.

"Are you saying you won't take me, Rush? I have no father here to take me. You're the only brother I have. My escort has to be a family member who's also a member of the club. I have no one else. Just you." She wasn't yelling anymore. She sounded hurt. The lost little girl who needed her big brother to save the day.

"Of course, I'm going to take you, Nan. I just forgot. And you started yelling at me before I had any fucking coffee," I said, not wanting to see the sadness in her eyes.

She sniffed and nodded stiffly. "OK. Thank you," she said, then bent to pick up the bag she had thrown down. "After you have coffee and are less mean, could you please bring my other bags up?" she asked as she continued up the steps.

She didn't need me to answer. She knew I would do it. I went to the kitchen. I had to get my anger under control. Going to this thing tonight mad wasn't fair to Nan. It was just one night. I would explain it to Blaire. She would understand, because she was . . . Blaire. She didn't expect me to do any-thing. She didn't require anything from me. She was the first person in my life to just want me for me. Not for favors.

My chest tightened. She would probably be asleep by the time I got home. I wanted her in my bed. I didn't want her going to sleep in the other bedroom. I wasn't sleeping without her.

I poured my coffee and downed it, then poured another cup, before heading back to the foyer to pick up all the shit Nan had brought in. She was coming down the stairs when I started up.

"Do you have the combination to Mom's jewelry box? I want to wear her sapphire necklace that she bought at Tiffany's that Christmas."

"I'll unlock it for you." I wasn't going to tell her to call Mom. There was a good chance Mom would say no, and then

Nan would break down, and I would have to clean that mess up, too.

Nan grinned. "Thank you! I'm going to wear one of the Marc Jacobs dresses, and that necklace will go perfectly. I think she bought those earrings that go so well with them, too. Or she borrowed them." Nan waved a hand as if it didn't matter. "No biggie. The necklace will go with the diamond teardrops."

I left her prattling about jewelry, took the bags to Mom's room, and dropped them on the bed. I had several tuxes here; I would just pick one. What I was wearing wasn't an issue. But I needed to talk to Blaire first. Let her know where I would be tonight.

It turned out she'd be working. My calls had gone straight to her voice mail, which meant her phone had been off or dead, which wasn't surprising, knowing Blaire and the importance she put on having a cell phone. When I had called the club, I had gotten Woods on the phone. He'd informed me that Blaire was busy. They were slammed getting ready for tonight. Then he'd told me Blaire would be working and warned me that if Nan said one thing to Blaire, he would have her escorted out. Then he'd hung up on me.

Fucker.

I was arriving at the club in a tux and with my sister on my arm, dressed like a princess. Dealing with the fact that Blaire would be serving tonight while I stood there dressed like this, highlighting our differences, was screwing with my head. I fucking hated this. I wanted Blaire in a dress that I'd paid a ridiculous amount of money for and smiling with excitement. I wanted the world to see that she was mine. That she was with me. But tonight was about my sister. If I could just get through it, then I would never be in this position again. Blaire would never serve at another event that I was attending. She'd be on my fucking arm, where she belonged.

"Remember what I said about Blaire. You do not speak to her unless you are going to say something nice. Woods will have you escorted out, and I will help him. Do you get me? I'm not blowing smoke, Nan."

Nan nodded stiffly. "I won't say a thing to her. I swear. Now, could you please stop making this about her and let me enjoy my night? You haven't even said anything about the way I look."

She was beautiful, but she was always beautiful. Nan had an elegant beauty that was impossible to hide. "You look gorgeous. No one will compare," I assured her.

She beamed at me, and I felt guilty for not thinking about the fact that I hadn't mentioned how she looked earlier. I had been so focused on Blaire that I hadn't thought about it. Nan needed me tonight. I had to think about her. For a few hours. This was for Nan. "Thank you," she said, smiling like the princess she knew she was.

"Let's go," I said, holding out my elbow for her to take. We walked up to the entrance, and a man in a tux smiled at us and nodded. He announced our names as we stepped into the room. All eyes turned to us. This was Nan's moment. She wanted to blow the other girls out of the water on first impression, and she did. I had no doubt.

When Nan saw one of her friends, she squeezed my arm

and went to join her. If only that was it. I had three more hours of this shit.

"You spoke to her?" Woods said, stopping beside me.

I nodded. "She'll be on her best behavior. If she says one thing, I will help you escort her out. She knows that."

Woods looked over the room and nodded. He started to leave but stopped and fidgeted with his cuff links before looking at me. "I hope you know what you're doing," he said simply, then walked off to greet some of the older members standing nearby. Woods was here as a host tonight. He wasn't with anyone.

I didn't let his words bother me. He was bitter, because I had been the one Blaire chose. I wouldn't let his comments get to me. I had to prepare myself to see Blaire working. Serving these pompous assholes and their spoiled daughters.

I made my way over to the farthest wall and hoped I wouldn't have to talk to too many of these people. Several stopped and spoke to me, and I nodded, forcing a smile. Glancing at my phone, I realized I had two hours and forty-five minutes left.

Then I saw her. She walked into the room, holding champagne flutes and with a smile on her face. The entire room seemed to light up with her presence. The members either ignored her and took a drink or spoke to her with a friendly smile. I realized most of the older golfers wanted to speak to her. She was popular with them, no doubt. Their wives even smiled fondly at her.

Once she was finished circling the room, she left, and I felt lost. She hadn't seen me, nor had she seemed to be looking for me. I had hoped she would scan the crowd for me. But she hadn't. Not once. Did she not want to see me? Did she think I didn't want to see her? Fuck . . . did she not know I was here? Would seeing me with Nan be a surprise? Hadn't Woods told her I'd be here?

Before I could get too worked up, Blaire walked back into the room, carrying a tray of martinis this time. She made another round. When she finally turned and her eyes met mine, I felt like my breath left me. A small smile touched her lips, and I fought the urge to take the damn tray out of her hands and shove it at the people reaching for drinks. I forced a smile I didn't feel, and then someone spoke to her, and she turned to smile at them. She didn't look back my way again before she left the room.

"Rush," Nan called. I saw her motioning me over to where she was standing. She was with the Drummonds and their daughter, Paris. Nan and Paris had gone to boarding school together. I was sure that at some point, I had made out with Paris when she had been at our house. I wasn't sure we had actually had sex. She'd still been seventeen, and I didn't mess with the illegal ones.

Nan grabbed my arm as I approached and reintroduced me to people I had already met. I nodded and listened to Nan and Paris talk about their last skiing trip together. When Nan tensed beside me, I turned to look at the door, knowing Blaire must have entered the room. Bethy was talking to Blaire, but Bethy wasn't working. She was dressed up. Confused, I watched as Jace stepped from a crowd to join Bethy.

He'd brought Bethy as his date.

I hadn't expected that. He was making a statement that she was more than a fuck for him. The smile on Blaire's face didn't surprise me. She was never jealous. She was happy for people.

Bethy was here as a guest because Jace had brought her, but Blaire was serving people, while I stood in a fucking tux.

Did she think I didn't want to acknowledge her as anything more than just a fuck? My stomach felt sick. She had to know the truth. Blaire never looked my way, but she knew I was watching her. The tense set of her shoulders told me she was ignoring me. Shit. Motherfucker.

She was reading the wrong thing into this. I hadn't wanted to come. I was here to escort my sister. I wasn't *not* acknowledging her. I was protecting her from Nan, but I wouldn't keep doing that if it meant I was hurting Blaire.

"Isn't that right, Rush?" Nan said, her overly bright voice sounding too high-pitched. She was pissed. She didn't want me watching Blaire, and that made me angry. I was here with Nan like she wanted. I was pretty sure she was wearing about ten grand's worth of clothing and accessories I had paid for, not counting our mother's necklace. And she was going to control whom I watched and spoke to? Fuck, no. She wasn't.

"Excuse me," I said, meaning to walk away, but Nan's nails dug into my arm.

"I was just saying that Mom and Abe should be home soon from Paris. They can't honeymoon forever," she said with a fake smile.

I didn't want them home. "I hope not," I said. Nan's nails dug deeper into my arm. I jerked free of her death grip.

She laughed and slapped at my arm. "He's a grouch at these things. Doesn't do tuxes well."

"He's a rock star's son. I doubt that requires you to wear a tux often," Mr. Drummond said in an amused tone.

I didn't point out to him that my rock-star father could

buy him and his company several times over. I wasn't going to waste my breath. "No. Not a lot of reasons to wear one."

"What is Laney saying to that server? She looks like she's about to—" Paris slammed her hand over her mouth, and I turned to see what was going on.

Blaire stood in the middle of the room with escargots all over the front of her clothing, and the tray she'd been carrying clattered loudly at her feet. She was frozen with shock and horror. Laney, Nan's friend, was cackling with laughter.

"Oh, and look, she's super clumsy. Woods should be pickier about his employees," Laney said loudly.

Nan's hand grabbed my arm, but I threw her off and stalked toward Blaire. That Laney bitch would pay for this.

"Move," I roared, shoving Laney and her friends out of my way so I could get to Blaire. Grabbing her by the waist, I stared down at her. "Are you OK?" I asked, checking for any harm done to her body other than the buttery slime all over her. She nodded, but her eyes were glistening with unshed tears, and I was ready to start tearing limbs from bodies. No one was allowed to touch her. No one. I couldn't turn to look completely at Laney. I was too close to hurting her. "Don't come near me or her again. Understood?" I said in a voice meant for Laney and anyone else standing around who thought messing with Blaire was acceptable.

"What are you mad at me for? She's the clumsy one. She dumped the whole tray all over herself," Laney said in a high-pitched, annoying voice. God, she was a bitch.

"If you utter one more word, I'll threaten to remove all my contributions from this club until you are escorted out. Permanently," I warned her.

"But I'm Nan's friend, Rush. Her oldest friend. You wouldn't do that to me. Especially for the hired help." Laney sounded shocked. I was about to give her something to be shocked about.

"Test me," I said, leveling my furious glare on her so she knew not to go there with me. I turned back to Blaire. "You're coming with me," I told her.

I glanced back to see Bethy standing there, ready to take Laney down right in front of everyone. "I have her, Bethy. She's OK. Go on back to Jace," I said. Then I turned back to Blaire. "Watch out for the snails; they're slippery." I had to get her out of here. Safely. She had gotten hurt. I hadn't protected her again. I should have been here with her. I fucked up. This was my fault. I always failed her.

When we stepped out of the ballroom and into the dark hallway that led back to the kitchen and offices, Blaire broke free from my hold and moved away from me. She crossed her arms over her chest in a defensive move. She was upset. I had let this happen.

"Blaire, I'm sorry. I wasn't expecting something like that to happen. I didn't even know she had issues with you. I'm going to talk to Nan about this. I have a feeling she had something to do with it—"

"The redhead hates me because of Woods's interest in me. Nan had nothing to do with it, and neither did you."

That didn't make sense. Why was Laney pissed over Woods? "Is Woods still hitting on you?" Blaire's eyes went wide, and she spun around and started to leave. I reached out and grabbed her arm. That was the wrong thing to say. Damn jealousy. I had to get a grip on that. "Blaire, wait. I'm sorry. I shouldn't have asked that. That isn't the issue right now. I wanted to make sure you were OK and help get you cleaned up." It sounded like I was begging, which I was, to an extent.

She let out a sigh, and her shoulders slumped. "I'm fine. I need to go to the kitchen and see if I even still have a job. I was warned by Woods this morning that something like this might happen and it would be my fault. So right now, I have bigger problems than you suddenly feeling the need to be possessive of me. Which is ridiculous. Because you were doing your best to ignore me until this incident happened. You either know me or you don't, Rush. Pick a team." She jerked her hand from mine and started toward the kitchen again. She was mad because I had ignored her? I had watched her every move, dammit.

"You were working. What did you want me to do?" I asked her. She stopped, and I took my chance to defend my actions. "Acknowledging you would have given Nan reason to attack you. I was protecting you."

Blaire's shoulders sagged. "You're right, Rush. You ignoring me would keep Nan from attacking me. I'm just the girl you fucked the past two nights. All things considered, I'm not that special. I'm one of many." Then she ran from me.

I stood there, frozen, so damn confused. The sound of the doors slamming echoed down the hallway. She was hurt. I had been doing what I thought she wanted me to do, and I'd hurt her.

Did she really think she was just some girl I fucked? God, how could she not see what she meant to me? I was so completely obsessed with her that she controlled every decision I made. What the hell did she expect from me? I loved her, dammit!

Chapter Twenty-Six

Nan came stalking out of the ballroom. Her eyes found me standing there alone, and the fury I knew was boiling under the surface exploded. "How could you do this to me?" she demanded. "This was my night. I just needed you to ignore her for one night, and you couldn't do it. Not even for an hour!"

"Just stop," I said, holding my hand up. I wasn't ready for this. I had to find Blaire.

"Don't tell me to stop. You humiliated me in there. You threatened my friend, a member of this club, because a server was clumsy!"

I took a step toward Nan. "Laney dumped that tray on her. You know it. Paris saw it. Bethy saw it. Do *not* correct me."

Footsteps interrupted me before I could say anything more. I turned to see Blaire, still covered in that crap, looking like she wanted to crawl into the nearest hole. She hurried away toward the door leading outside.

"Blaire, wait," I called after her. I had to talk to her.

"Let her go, Rush," Nan demanded.

"I can't," I replied, and took off running after Blaire.

The door closed behind Blaire, but I shoved it open and followed her out.

"Blaire, please wait. Talk to me," I begged.

She stopped walking, and I caught up to her. She was giving me a chance.

"I'm sorry, but you're wrong. I didn't ignore you in there. Go ask anyone. My eyes never left you. If there was any question in anyone's mind how I felt about you, the fact that I couldn't look away from you while you walked around that room should have answered it." I had to say this right. I couldn't fuck this up. I needed her to understand how I felt. "Then I saw the look on your face when you saw Bethy with Jace. Something inside me was ripped open. I didn't know what you were thinking, but I knew you had realized the wrongness of tonight. You should have never been there serving anyone. You should have been by my side. I wanted you beside me. I was strung so damn tight waiting for anyone to make a wrong move toward you that I forgot to breathe most of the time."

My gaze fell to her clenched fists at her sides. I hated seeing her like this. I ran my finger over her hand.

"If you can forgive me, I promise this will never happen again. I love Nan. But I'm done trying to please her. She's my sister, but she has some issues she needs to work out. I've told her that I'm going to talk to you about everything. There are some things you need to know." I hadn't meant to say that, but I had to. I was going to lose her if I didn't tell her now. I would tell her I loved her first. I wanted her to know that. "I'm dealing with the fact that you may walk away from me once you know them and never look back. It scares the hell out of me. I don't know what this is that is going on between us, but from the moment I laid eyes on you, I knew you were going to change my world. I was terrified. The more I watched you, the more you drew me in. I couldn't get close enough."

"OK," she said simply.

What did that mean? "OK?" I asked.

She nodded. "OK. If you actually want to keep me so badly that you're willing to open up to me, then OK."

A grin touched my lips. Damn, she always made me smile. "I just bared my soul to you, and all I get is an 'OK'?" I asked.

"You said everything I needed to hear. I'm hooked now. You have me. What are you going to do with me?"

The relief that ran through me made my knees go weak. I had to keep my cool. I couldn't scare her with my intensity. Hell, it scared me. "I'm thinking sex on the sixteenth hole by the lake would be nice."

Blaire tilted her head to the side and acted like she was considering it. "Hmmm . . . problem is, I'm supposed to change and go work in the kitchen the rest of the night."

Not what I wanted to hear. "Shit."

She stepped closer to me and pressed a kiss to my jaw. "You have a sister to escort," she said.

I wasn't going to make it through tonight. "All I can think about is being inside you. Having you pressed close to me and hearing you make those sexy-ass little moans."

Desire flickered in Blaire's eyes as her pupils dilated.

I decided to keep talking, since she liked it. "If I could walk away from you easily, I'd take you into that office and press you up against the wall and bury myself deep inside. But I can't have a quickie with you. You're too damn addictive."

Blaire's hands were still on my shoulders. She squeezed them, and her breathing hitched.

"Go change. I'll stand out here so I'm not tempted. Then I'll walk you back to the kitchen," I told her.

She took a deep breath, then stepped back and went in to change.

The temptation to go in there with her and make love to her before sending her back to work was hard to ignore. But she wanted to finish working tonight. It was important to her. I wanted to prove to her that what was important to her was important to me.

When she walked back out, she was wearing a clean cart-girl uniform and smiling at me.

"Sure you don't want to take me back to the sixteenth hole? I promise I'll be quick. Just let me lick your pussy until you come."

Blaire trembled and let out a shaky breath. "Rush, don't say that. I can't. I have to go back to work, and I don't want Jimmy wondering why I'm a jumble of nerves."

Smiling, I reached for her hand and threaded my fingers through hers. "You clean up well," I told her teasingly.

Blaire giggled. "I sure smell better now, too," she said.

I tugged her over to my side and ducked my head to inhale her. "You always smell amazing, sweet Blaire."

She leaned into me, and I moved my hand to tuck her beside me as I walked her back into the building and to the kitchen door.

"I'm gonna kiss you. I know you're at work, but right now, I just don't care. I need to taste you." I leaned down to press my lips against hers. I licked her bottom lip, pulled it into my mouth and sucked, then let it go with a reluctant peck.

Blaire shot me one last grin before leaving me standing there without her.

◇

Going through the motions and finishing the night had been hell. But I'd made it, and Nan seemed happy. She chatted on the way back to the house about a shopping trip she wanted to take with Paris and asked if I had talked to Mom lately.

When Nan had driven away, I let out a sigh of relief and went inside the house. Blaire would be home soon, and I was still giving her that massage. She more than needed it now. She'd been going all damn day.

I walked through the kitchen on my way to the stairs. The empty bottle of beer and the wineglass sitting on the bar stopped me in my tracks. At that moment, the world felt like it had ceased spinning and I was moving in slow motion toward the glass.

Familiar red lipstick on the glass made my stomach turn. Fuck, no. Not yet. God, not yet. I needed tonight. Motherfucker. I needed one more night. She wasn't ready. I had to plan this. Shit!

I headed for the stairs and took them two at a time, needing to see for myself. As I walked down the hall, I saw that the door to my mother's room was closed. They were in there. I knew they were. That door was normally open. I didn't touch the door. I was afraid to see them. I was afraid they would destroy this. They would tell her everything and send her away from me.

No.

God, no.

No, no, no.

◇

She didn't come home for hours. I didn't know how many; I just knew it was late. I had been sitting outside my door on the floor, waiting for her. Staring straight ahead. Needing to see her and hold her and know she was here with me. She wasn't gone.

The sound of the front door opening sent my heart into a wild frenzy. Blaire was home. This could be it. The end. No. No. No. I wouldn't allow it. I would make her love me. Make her forgive me.

When she stopped on the top step and saw me, I sat there and took her in. My sweet Blaire. She had shown up and stolen a piece of my heart without opening her mouth. Then she'd consumed me. Taken it all. I had let her have it freely.

She started walking toward me, and I stood up and went to her. "I need you upstairs. Now." The desperation in my voice seemed to surprise her, but she didn't question me.

I grabbed her hand and pulled her toward my door. I had to hurry and get her tucked safely into my room. Away from them. I tugged her inside and closed the door, before turning to her and pressing her against the wall.

I ran my hands down her body, memorizing each curve. It wasn't enough. I needed the clothes off. Grabbing the front of the shirt she was wearing, I ripped it open. I didn't have time for buttons. She gasped, and I covered her mouth with mine. I stabbed her sweet warmth with my tongue over and over, while I made quick work of the snap of her shorts and jerked them down her legs. She was naked. My Blaire. My perfect, sweet Blaire.

Growling against her mouth, I knew I needed more. She wasn't leaving me. I couldn't let her leave me. I pushed her back onto the steps and jerked her shoes off, then pulled her shorts and panties the rest of the way off. Completely naked. Just for me to see. No one else. Ever. Just for me.

Falling to my knees, I pushed her legs apart and ran my tongue up her slit, lapping at the clit that was already swollen and ready for me. Blaire cried out my name and fell back on her elbows. Her thighs fell open more as I slid my tongue inside her, before running it along the tender folds again. My name was a chant on her lips. I began kissing the soft skin of her thighs, and she trembled with needy whimpers.

"Mine. This is mine." Lifting my head, I looked at her. "Mine. This sweet pussy is mine, Blaire." It was mine.

She shuddered as I pressed my finger inside her heat.

"Tell me it's mine," I demanded.

She nodded as I slipped my finger further inside her.

"Tell me it's mine," I repeated.

"It's yours. Now, please, Rush, fuck me," she said, panting.

Yes! That was my girl. Yes, she was mine. She needed to know she was mine. This was mine. Standing up, I jerked down the pajama pants I'd been wearing and kicked them aside. "No condom tonight. I'll pull out. I just need to feel all of you," I told her.

I would never put a condom between us again. I never wanted to be separated from her. Grabbing her thighs, I moved her up as I shifted down and lined my cock up with her entrance. I couldn't slam into her if she was sore. God, she had to be so damn tired, but I had to have her. Slowly, I moved inside her.

"Does it hurt?" I asked, holding myself over her.

"It feels good," she said with a sigh.

I was going to hurt her. I stopped and pulled out. "These stairs are too hard for you. Come here."

I picked her up in my arms and carried her up the stairs. She was too fragile tonight to press against the hard wooden stairs.

"Will you do something for me?" I asked her, peppering kisses on her nose and eyelids while I stood beside my bed.

"Yes," she replied.

I set her down on the floor and held on to her, even after her feet touched the rug. "Bend over and lay your chest flat on the bed. Put your hands over your head, and leave your ass stuck up in the air."

I had fantasized about seeing her this way. She didn't ask why or argue. She simply did it. Knowing she wanted to please me so easily made the panic grow. She was it for me. She had to know that.

I ran my hand over the round, smooth ass that she so willingly presented to me. "You have the most perfect ass I've ever seen," I told her as I caressed it. Taking a firm hold of her hips and moving her legs farther apart, I entered her in one thrust.

"Rush!" Blaire cried out.

"Fuck, I'm deep." I groaned, and my eyes rolled back in my head. Better than I had imagined. It was always more with her. Always fucking more.

I began pumping inside her. She pressed back against me and grabbed handfuls of sheets as she made loud moans and pleas for more.

Hearing her pleasure made me push harder. I couldn't get

deep enough. I wanted to live in here. Locked inside her. The tight suction grabbed my cock, making my knees buckle. I was close. Reaching down between her legs, I slid my hand over her pussy. "God, you're soaking wet."

My words were all it took. Blaire bucked back against me wildly, calling out my name. It took all my control to pull out of her and shoot my release onto her ass. I wanted it inside her. My pleasure mixed with hers. But I couldn't do that again. Yet.

"Gaaaah!" I yelled, as my cock jerked in my hands and shot my load all over her smooth back. Seeing myself there made me feel like I had marked her. I could see it. Me all over her. "Damn, baby, if you only knew how fucking incredible your ass looks right now," I said.

She fell onto the bed, no longer able to hold herself up. She turned her head to the side to look at me. "Why?"

She didn't realize where I had shot my release. "Let's just say I need to clean you up," I explained.

A giggle burst out of her, and she buried her face in the covers.

I loved hearing her laugh. I also loved standing here and staring at her ass covered in my come. Those two things combined were pretty damn awesome.

She needed to sleep. I couldn't make her lie here with my come on her because I was a fucking caveman. Moving around her, I headed for the bathroom and got a warm, wet washcloth, then headed back into the room.

I could see her eyes follow me and the sleepy, satisfied smile on her face. I had put that smile there. I didn't know if she was supposed to work tomorrow or not, but she wasn't working. I would deal with it. I had to talk to her. She had to know.

Her dad was here. It was time I faced it and fought for her.

I cleaned the come off her bottom. "All clean, baby. You can crawl on up and get covered up. I'll be right back," I told her.

But she didn't move. I walked around and looked at her face. She was sound asleep. I smiled at the thought of her falling asleep while I was cleaning her up. The possessive beast within beat on his chest.

I picked her up and moved her to the pillow, then covered her carefully. Leaning down, I pressed a kiss to her head. "I will fix this. I swear I will make it right. I love you enough to get us through this. I just need *you* to love *me* enough. Please, Blaire. Love me enough," I pleaded.

She didn't move. Her slow, even breathing never changed. But I hoped she heard me in her sleep. And that tomorrow she would remember.

Chapter Twenty-Seven

I couldn't sleep. I lay there for hours, watching Blaire sleep in my arms. She had curled up against me and clung to me as if I were her only source of warmth. The fear that I might never have this again was very real. As much as I didn't want to believe she would leave me, I knew I could lose her. How would I survive that? I pulled her closer to me and held her tighter. If I could just take her and run away. Never let her know the awful truth. Why did I always have to hurt her, when all I wanted to do was protect her?

"I love you," I whispered into her hair.

That had to be enough for us.

I watched the sun come up and the morning grow brighter. Blaire needed sleep. She'd probably sleep until noon. I had to talk to my mother and Abe before Blaire woke up. They needed to know how I felt about her. She had become my top priority. That had to be made clear.

Closing my eyes, I inhaled her and soaked in the feel of her in my arms. So trusting. Forcing myself to get out of bed, I moved her over and out of my arms. I was ready to go downstairs and deal with the truth. The ugly, horrible, sordid truth that was going to hurt her. I couldn't stop that. I could just hope that I was enough to help her heal.

I pulled on my clothes and headed for the stairs, then stopped and looked back at Blaire lying in my bed. She was curled up in the covers now. Her long blond hair was fanned out over my pillow. As a child, I had often wondered if angels were real. By the time I was ten, I had decided they weren't. That was all bullshit. I realized now that I'd been wrong.

Blaire was my angel.

Abe was standing in the kitchen, drinking a cup of coffee and looking out the window. This was the man who had abandoned my Blaire. He'd let her bury her mother and left her to figure it out all on her own.

I hated him.

He didn't deserve Blaire.

Abe turned and met my glare. A frown tugged on his mouth, and he took another sip of coffee before turning to look out the window again. He was used to my hatred. But he had no idea how high it had risen since he'd seen me last. I wanted to start ripping his arms off his body. Just looking at him infuriated me.

"Are you going to ask about her?" I snarled.

He shrugged. "She's here, I assume." He assumed. He didn't care. He just assumed.

"What fucked you up so badly that you could be so heartless?" I asked, hate laced in my words.

"A pain like you could never understand, boy," he replied. His voice was empty of emotion.

"She buried her mother by herself, you son of a bitch. And you knew it."

He didn't reply.

"She is so fucking innocent and alone," I said, needing him to acknowledge her, or I was going to lose my shit.

"She isn't anymore, is she? Innocent and alone, that is," he said.

My anger hit a boiling point, and I moved across the kitchen. He turned just in time for me to grab him and throw him up against the wall. "You motherfucking piece of shit! Do not *ever*, and I fucking mean *ever*, insinuate for a minute that Blaire is anything less than innocent. I will end you! I don't give a fuck who wants you!" I was yelling.

Abe had dropped his coffee, and the cup had shattered on the floor, but I ignored it. He didn't look like he cared. There was an emptiness in this man that I didn't understand. It was as if he had no soul. "Did you sleep with her?" he said calmly.

I slammed him against the wall again, hard enough to rattle the walls and send plates falling to join the broken cup. "Shut up!" I roared.

"Rush!" My mother's hysterical voice broke through my rage.

"Not your business, Mom," I said, not taking my eyes off the man I was ready to murder with my bare hands.

"Doesn't sound like she's alone anymore, either," Abe said.

I swallowed the fear that was clawing at my chest. "She's not. She never will be. I'll always be there for her. I'll keep her safe. I'll take care of her. She will *always* have me."

"Who? What are you talking about, Rush? Let Abe go!" My mother was beside me, pulling on my arm.

Blaire was going to come downstairs soon. I couldn't kill her father. Not unless she asked me to. Then he was a dead man. I let go of him and stepped back. "Careful how you speak about her. I want nothing more than to see you suffer," I warned him.

"Rush, that is enough!" My mother's nails dug into my arm, and I jerked free of her.

"Don't you touch me, either. You wanted this sack of shit in our lives. You let him leave her." I pointed my finger at her.

My mother's shock grew to confusion as she looked around her at the broken things. "You've made a mess in here. Go into the living room before someone gets cut. I need an explanation for your behavior," she said, walking out of the room and expecting us to follow.

I watched her go, then looked over at Abe.

"Nothing you can do to me will compare to the suffering I've been through," Abe said, and then he turned and followed my mother out of the kitchen.

How did that man raise someone like Blaire? I didn't understand how that woman upstairs in my bed could be a product of this man. Nan I could see, but not Blaire.

I had to talk to my mother and Abe. It was why I had gotten up and left my bed with Blaire still tucked in it. I walked into the living room, and my mother looked at me with a gaping mouth. Apparently, Abe had told her something.

"You . . . you . . . I can't believe you, Rush. I know you have a problem with sleeping around, but you have to draw the line somewhere. That girl used her body to manipulate you."

I shook my head and stalked toward my mother. I was done with hearing them talk about Blaire. I no longer cared who the hell said it, they would pay.

Abe stepped between us, but his attention was on my

mother. "Be careful what you say about her. Blaire is my daughter." The warning in his tone surprised me. It didn't make up for his other shit, but he had defended her.

"I can't believe you, Rush. What were you thinking? You know who she is? What she means to this family?" my mother said in a horrified tone, like I had committed a crime. She blamed Blaire for something that was never her fault. How insane was this thought process my family believed in so much?

"You can't hold her responsible. She wasn't even born yet. You have no idea what all she's been through. What *he* has put her through," I said, pointing at Abe. Because I did know, and I would never forget it.

"Don't go getting all high and mighty. You were the one who went and found him for me. So whatever he put her through, you started it all. Then you go and *sleep* with her? Really, Rush. My God, what were you thinking? You're just like your father." My mother loved accusing me of being just like Dean when she was mad at me. I was just thankful that I was nothing like her.

"Remember who owns this house, Mother," I reminded her.

"Can you believe this? He's turning on me over a girl he just met. Abe, you have to do something."

My mother looked pleadingly at Abe, and I wanted to laugh. She expected him to do something. That was bullshit. I was tired of this. I needed to get this shit straightened out before Blaire woke up.

"It's his house, Georgie. I can't force him to do anything. I should have expected this. She's so much like her mother."

His words caused me to pause. What the hell did he mean by that?

"What is that supposed to mean?" my mother roared, obviously already knowing what he meant, or she wouldn't be about to lose it on him.

"We've been over this before. The reason I left you for her was that she had this draw to her. I couldn't seem to let her go—"

"I *know* that. I don't want to hear it again. You wanted her so damn badly you left me pregnant with a bunch of wedding invitations to rescind," my mother said, interrupting him.

"Sweetheart, calm down. I love you. I was just explaining that Blaire has her mother's charisma. It's impossible not to be drawn to her. And she's just as blind to it as her mother was. She can't help it," Abe said.

I stared at him in horror. Did he think that was it? Did he really believe that? I wasn't in love with fucking charisma. She was so much more. Didn't he see that? Blind bastard.

"Argh! Will that woman never leave me alone? Will she always ruin my life? She's gone, for crying out loud. I have the man I love back, and our daughter finally has her father, and now this. Rush goes and sleeps with this, this *girl*!" My mother was getting worked up, and I didn't have time for her temper tantrum. I had to worry about Blaire.

"One more word against her, and I will have you leave," I warned my mother for the last time. She was not going to disrespect Blaire in any way.

"Georgie, honey, please calm down. Blaire is a good girl. Her being here isn't the end of the world. She needs somewhere to stay. I explained this to you already. I know you hate Rebecca now, but she was your best friend. The two of you had been friends since you were kids. Until I came along and ruined everything, the two of you were like sisters. This is her daughter. Have some compassion." The reasoning he was throwing out there wasn't going to work on my mom. She was as insanely self-centered as my sister.

"No! Shut up, all of you!" Blaire's voice sent a blade straight through my heart.

No. God no, not yet. She wasn't supposed to hear it this way. "Blaire." I moved toward her, but she threw up her hands to hold me back. The wild look in her eyes as she looked right past me stopped me cold.

"You," she said, pointing her finger at Abe. "You are just letting them lie about my mother!" she yelled. I had been terrified that she would be hurt, but the complete, out-of-reach coldness in her eyes was terrifying.

"Blaire, let me explain—" Abe started to say.

"Shut up!" Blaire roared, interrupting him. "My sister, my other half, died. She died, Dad. In a car on her way to the store with *you*. It was like my soul had been taken from me and torn in two. Losing her was unbearable. I watched my mother wail and cry and mourn, and then I watched my father walk away, never to return, while his daughter and wife were trying to pick up the pieces of their world without Valerie in it. Then my mother got sick. I called you, but you didn't answer. So I got an extra job after school, and I started making payments for Mom's medical care. I did nothing but care for my mother and go to school. Except that in my senior year, she got so sick that I had to drop out. Took my GED and was done with it. Because the only person on the planet who loved me was dying as I sat and watched helplessly. I held her hand while she took her last breath. I arranged her funeral. I watched them lower her into the ground. You never once called. Not once. Then I had to sell the house Gran left us and everything of value in it just to pay off medical bills." She stopped talking, and a sob escaped her. Tears were streaming down her face, and my heart exploded.

I hadn't known all of that. She had only told me a little. I wrapped my arms around her, needing to hold her, but she began swinging and fighting against me like someone who had lost her mind.

"Don't touch me!" she screamed, and I had to let her go or risk her hurting herself. "Now I'm being forced to hear you talk about my mother, who was a saint. Do you hear me? She was a saint! You are all *liars*. If anyone is guilty of this bullshit I hear pouring out of your mouth, it is that man." She pointed at her father.

I had kidded myself to think she would listen and let me explain. Her world was being turned upside down with this news. I hadn't told her. I hadn't wanted to see the look of pain in her eyes, which I didn't know how to ease. But I had let this happen instead, and it was so much worse.

"He is the liar. He isn't worth the dirt beneath my feet. If Nan is his daughter, if you were pregnant . . ." Blaire had been pointing at Abe as she spoke, but she stopped and moved her attention to my mother.

For the first time, she actually looked at my mother. And she remembered. She staggered back, and I wanted to reach out and hold her again, but I didn't. She needed to get control on her own first. She didn't want my help.

"Who are you?" she asked, as my mother stared at her with a haunted look in her eyes.

"Careful how you answer that," I warned my mother, after I stepped up behind Blaire, just in case she needed me.

My mother looked at Abe and then back to Blaire. "You know who I am, Blaire. We've met before."

"You came to my house. You . . . you made my mother cry."

My mother rolled her eyes, and I tensed.

"Last warning, Mother," I growled.

"Nan wanted to meet her father. So I brought her to him. She got to see his nice little family, with the pretty blond twin daughters he loved and an equally perfect wife. I was tired of having to tell my daughter she didn't have a father. She knew she did. So I showed her just what he had chosen instead of her. She didn't ask about him again until much later in life."

Blaire's knees went weak, and she gasped for air. Shit, she was going to have a panic attack.

"Blaire, please, look at me," I begged her, but she didn't respond. She kept her gaze on the ground as everything slowly sank in for her. I hated watching this. I wanted to order them all out of here so I could hold Blaire until everything was right again. But she needed this. It was out there. She wanted her answers.

Abe spoke. "I was engaged to Georgianna. She was pregnant with Nan. Your mother came to visit her. She was like no one I'd ever met. She was addictive. I couldn't seem to stay away from her. Georgianna was still pining over Dean, and Rush was still visiting his dad every other weekend. I expected Georgie to go to Dean the minute he decided he wanted a family. I wasn't even sure Nan was mine. Your mother was innocent and fun. She wasn't into rockers, and she made me laugh. I pursued her, and she ignored me. Then I lied to her. I told her Georgie was pregnant with another of Dean's kids. She felt sorry for me. I somehow persuaded her to run away with me. To throw away a friendship she'd had all her life." When Abe finished his explanation, I realized that was the most I had ever heard him say at one time.

Blaire covered her ears and closed her eyes tightly. "Stop. I don't want to hear it. I just want my things. I just want to leave." Blaire sobbed, ripping me in two.

"Baby, please talk to me. Please." I pleaded with her and touched her arms, needing some form of connection to her.

She moved away from me, but she didn't look at me. "I can't look at you. I don't want to talk to you. I just want my things. I want to go home."

No. No. No. I couldn't lose her. No. She wasn't leaving me. I loved her. She owned me. She had to fight for us. I needed her to fight.

"Blaire, honey, there *is* no home," Abe said. I knew he meant to remind her that she had nowhere to go, but I wanted to bury my fist in his face. She didn't need to hear that from him right now.

Blaire glared at her father. "My mother's and my sister's graves are home. I want to be near them. I've stood here and listened to y'all tell me my mother was someone I know she wasn't. She would have never done what you're accusing her of. Stay here with your family, Abe. I'm sure they will love you as much as your last one did. Try not to kill any of them," she said in words laced with hatred.

Then she turned and fled up the stairs. I stared at her and considered locking her in my room and forcing her to stay with me. To listen to me. Would she forgive me then? Could I do that to her?

"She's unstable and dangerous," my mother hissed.

I stalked over to her and got up in her face for the first time I my life. "Her world was just ripped away from her. Everything she's known. So for once in your life, don't be a selfish bitch, and shut the hell up. Because I am ready to throw you both out and let you figure out a way to fucking survive on your own."

I didn't wait to listen to her response, because I knew it would push me over the edge. I had to try to talk to Blaire without her father and my mother in the way.

I stood in the doorway of her room as she crammed her clothing into the suitcase she had arrived with only weeks ago.

"You can't leave me," I said, fighting the emotion clogging my throat.

"Watch me," she replied.

The emptiness in her voice was killing me. That wasn't my Blaire. I wouldn't let this lie take her from me. My Blaire wasn't so lifeless and cold inside.

"Blaire, you didn't let me explain. I was going to tell you everything today. They came home last night, and I panicked. I needed to tell you first." I wasn't making sense, and she was leaving, but I didn't know what the fuck to say to get her to stay. Slamming my fist against the doorframe, I tried to focus. I had to say the right thing. "You were not supposed to find out that way. Not like that. God, not like that." I was losing it. The panic and fear were hindering my thoughts.

"I can't stay here," she said. "I can't see you. You represent the pain and betrayal of not just me but my mom. Whatever we had is over. It died the minute I walked downstairs and realized the world I'd always known was a lie."

Her words were so final. How could I fight if she refused to give us a chance? Would she never be able to look at me any other way again? I couldn't live in a world like that. One without Blaire.

Chapter Twenty-Eight

Fighting to breathe through the pain, I turned and followed her. She didn't want me. She didn't want this. But I couldn't just let her go. Where would she go? Where would she sleep? Who would make sure she ate? Who would hold her when she cried? She needed me. And God, I needed her.

Blaire reached the bottom step, took the phone out of her pocket, and shoved it at Abe. "Take it. I don't want it," she said.

"Why would I take your phone?" Abe asked.

"Because I don't want anything from you," she yelled at him.

"I didn't give you that phone," he said.

"Take the phone, Blaire," I said. "If you want to leave, I can't hold you here. But please, take the phone." I was ready to get on my knees and beg. She had to take that phone. Dammit, she needed a phone.

Blaire laid it down on the bottom step. "I can't," she said, and I knew I couldn't make her take it, either. I couldn't do anything. I was fucking useless. Her world had just been blown to pieces, and I was fucking useless.

"You look just like her," my mother said to Blaire's back.

"I only hope I can be half the woman she was," Blaire said, with complete conviction in her voice.

The door closed behind her.

I had to do something.

I moved down the stairs, not taking my eyes off the door. I couldn't just stay here and let her drive away. "Where will she go?" I asked Abe. He would have an idea.

"She'll go back to Alabama. The only other home she knows. She has friends there. They will take her in," he said.

Nan's scream came from outside, and my heart stopped. Had something happened to Blaire? I ran down the stairs, but not before my mother and Abe had bounded out the door.

"Blaire! Put the gun down. Nan, don't move. She knows how to use that thing better than most men," Abe ordered in a calm voice.

Holy shit, Blaire was holding a gun on Nan. What the fuck had Nan said?

"What is she doing with that thing? Is that even legal for her to have?" my mother asked.

"She has a permit, and she knows what she's doing. Stay calm," Abe said, sounding annoyed.

Blaire lowered the gun. "I'm gonna get in that truck and drive out of your life. Forever. Just keep your mouth shut about my momma. I won't listen to it again," Blaire said, glaring at Nan. Then she climbed inside the truck, and without a backward glance, she drove away.

"She's fucking insane," Nan said, turning to look back at us.

I couldn't stand out here and listen to them. She was leaving me. I couldn't just let her go alone. Anything could happen to her. I turned and went inside and up to my room.

The smell of Blaire hit me as I reached the top step, and I

had to stop and grit my teeth through the pain. Just two hours ago, I had lain in that bed and held her in my arms.

I walked over to the bed, sat down, and picked up the pillow she'd been sleeping on and held it to my face. God, it smelled just like her. A sob broke free, and I fought to keep it back, but I couldn't. I had lost her. My Blaire. I had lost my Blaire.

No. No. I wasn't accepting that.

I stood up and laid the pillow back down reverently. I was going after her. I needed some clothes and my wallet. I was going to get her. She needed me. She didn't want me right now, but she would after the shock wore off. I could hold her and ease her pain. I would hold her while she cried. Then I would spend my life making things right. Making her happy. So fucking happy.

I walked back down the stairs with my bag in my hands, while my mother, my sister, and Abe stood in the foyer talking about Blaire and what had happened, I was sure. I wasn't listening to them. I was leaving.

"Where are you going?" my mother asked me.

"She held a gun to my head, Rush! Do you not care about that? She could have killed me!" Nan knew where I was going.

I stopped and looked at my mother first. "I'm going to get Blaire." Then I looked at my sister. "You will learn to shut your fucking mouth. You said the wrong thing to the wrong person this time, and you learned a lesson. Next time, think before you spew shit." I jerked the door open.

"What if she won't come back with you? She hates us, Rush," my mother said, sounding annoyed at the idea of her even coming here.

"If she won't come back with me, then you all will have to move out. I will not live in *my house* with the people who destroyed her world. Decide where you plan to go, because I don't want you here when I return." I slammed the door behind me.

The eight-hour drive to Summit, Alabama, would have been easier if I hadn't been tailing Blaire and also trying to keep her from seeing me. Hiding a black Range Rover on country roads wasn't easy. I had to let her get out of sight more times than I wanted, but it was the only way to follow her. I had the small town plugged into my GPS, and luckily, Blaire seemed to be taking the same route the GPS suggested.

When I entered the small town, I saw that the *Welcome to Summit, Alabama*, sign was worn and in need of some new paint, but you could make out what it said well enough. I had let her get a good ten minutes ahead of me, because it was the only way to stay out of her sight. I pulled through the first traffic light. According to Google, this town had only three traffic lights. At the next one, I saw the cemetery sign and turned. The parking lot was empty except for Blaire's truck and another truck. I didn't park where she could see me; I made sure to park down the road a bit.

She had come to see her mother. And her sister. Had my heart ever truly broken for someone else like this? I had hated how Nan was neglected, but had I ever felt this kind of emotion for her pain? The idea of Blaire dealing with this alone was too much. She had to listen to me.

When I saw her blue truck move, I waited until I was sure

it had pulled back onto the road before following at a safe distance. She turned right at the first traffic light and then parked at a motel. I was sure it was the only motel for miles and miles. As much as I hated the idea of her staying here, I was glad I wouldn't have to do this at some stranger's house. We had privacy here.

While she was inside getting a room, I parked my car and got out and waited. I wasn't sure what I was going to say or if I was just going to beg. But I had to do something. Blaire stepped back out of the office, and her eyes locked with mine. Her step faltered, and then she sighed. She hadn't expected me to follow her. Again, did she not understand how fucking crazy I was about her?

A car door slammed just as she started walking toward me, and she turned her head and frowned at the guy who had just climbed out of the truck, the same one I'd just seen at the cemetery. I knew without an introduction that the guy was Cain. The possessive way he watched her told me that he'd once had a claim on her. He just needed to know that the claim was no longer valid.

"I'm hoping like hell you know this guy, 'cause he followed you here from the cemetery. I noticed him on the side of the road watching us a ways back, but I didn't say anything," Cain said as he sauntered over to stand in front of Blaire.

"I know him," Blaire said without pause.

"He the reason you came running home?" Cain asked.

"No," she said, then looked back at me. "Why are you here?" she asked me, without coming any closer.

"You're here," I replied simply.

"I can't do this, Rush."

Yes, she could. I had to get her to see that. I took a step toward her. "Talk to me. Please, Blaire. There is so much I need to explain."

She shook her head and backed up. "No. I can't."

I wanted to bash in Cain's head. "Could you give us a minute?" I asked him.

He crossed his arms over his chest and stepped completely in front of her. "I don't think so. It doesn't seem like she wants to talk to you. Can't say I'm gonna make her. And neither are you."

I had started to move toward him when Blaire moved out from behind him. "It's OK, Cain. This is my stepbrother, Rush Finlay. He already knows who you are. He wants to talk. So we are going to talk. You can leave. I'll be fine," she said over her shoulder, before unlocking room 4A.

She had just called me her stepbrother. What the fuck?

"Stepbrother? Wait . . . Rush Finlay? As in Dean Finlay's only child? Shit, B, you're related to a rock celebrity," Cain said, his mouth going slack as he stared at me.

Just what I needed, a big enough Slacker Demon fan to know Dean's son's name.

"Go, Cain," she said sternly, then stepped inside the room.

Chapter Twenty-Nine

Blaire walked into the room and went to the farthest corner before turning around. "Talk. Hurry. I want you gone," she said in a tight voice.

"I love you." I should have told her already. I should have told her yesterday. I should have fucking told her the moment I realized it, but I hadn't.

She started shaking her head. She wasn't going to listen to me. I was going to have to fucking beg. I would fight enough for both of us.

"I know my actions don't appear to back that up, but if you'd just let me explain. God, baby, I can't stand seeing you in so much pain," I said, pleading.

"Nothing you can say will fix this. She was my mother, Rush. The one memory that holds anything good in my life. She is the center of every happy childhood moment I had. And you . . ." She paused and closed her eyes. "And you, and . . . and them. Y'all disgraced her. The ugly lies that you spoke as if they were the truth."

I hated myself. I hated the lies. I hated my mother and Abe.

"I'm so sorry you found out this way. I wanted to tell you. At first, you were just a problem that would hurt Nan. I thought you'd cause her more pain. The trouble was that you fascinated me. I'll admit I was immediately drawn to you because you're gorgeous. Breathtaking. I hated you because of it. I didn't want to be attracted to you. But I was. I wanted you badly that very first night. Just to be near you. God, I made up reasons to find you. Then . . . then I got to know you. I was hypnotized by your laugh. It was the most amazing sound I'd ever heard. You were so honest and determined. You didn't whine or complain. You took what life handed you and worked with it. I wasn't used to that. Every time I watched you, every time I was near you, I fell a little more."

I took a step toward her, and she held up her hands as if to keep me back. I had to keep talking. I needed her to believe me.

"Then that night at the honky-tonk. You owned me after that. You may not have realized it, but I was hooked. There was no going back for me. I had so much to make up for. I'd put you through hell since you'd arrived, and I hated myself for it. I wanted to give you the world. But I knew . . . I knew who you were. When I let myself remember exactly who you were, I would pull back. How could I be so completely wrapped up in the girl who represented my sister's pain?"

Blaire covered her ears. "No. I won't listen to this. Leave, Rush. Leave now!" she yelled.

"The day Mom came home from the hospital with her, I was three. I remember it, though. She was so small, and I remember worrying that something would happen to her. My mom cried a lot. So did Nan. I grew up fast. By the time Nan was three, I was doing everything from fixing her breakfast to tucking her in at night. Our mom had married, and now we had Grant. There was never any stability. I actually looked forward to the times my dad would come get me, because I wouldn't be responsible for Nan for a few days. I'd get a break. Then she began asking why I had a daddy and she didn't." I needed Blaire to understand why I did what I did. It had been wrong, but she had to understand.

"Stop!" she yelled, moving back farther against the wall.

"Blaire, I need you to hear me. This is the only way you'll understand," I begged. The sob in my throat caused my voice to crack, but I wasn't stopping. She had to listen to me. "Mom would tell her she didn't have one because she was special. That didn't work for very long. I demanded that Mom tell me who Nan's dad was. I wanted it to be mine. I knew my dad would take her places. Mom told me that Nan's dad had another family. He had two little girls he loved more than Nan. He wanted those girls, but he didn't want Nan. I couldn't understand how anyone couldn't want Nan. She was my little sister. Sure, at times I wanted to kill her, but I loved her fiercely. Then came the day Mom took her to see the family her father had chosen. Nan cried for months afterward."

I stopped talking, and Blaire sank down onto the bed. She was giving in and listening to me. I felt a small glimmer of hope.

"I hated those girls. I hated that family Nan's dad had chosen over her. I swore that one day, I'd make him pay. Nan would always say that maybe one day, he'd come see her. She daydreamed about him wanting to see her. I listened to these daydreams for years. When I was nineteen I went looking for him. I knew his name. I found him. I left him a picture of Nan with our address on the back. I told him he had another daughter who was special, and she just wanted to meet him. To talk to him."

I could see her do the math in her head. She'd lost her sister less than a year before I'd found Abe. But I hadn't known. God, I'd had no idea. I had been trying to help my sister, not destroy Blaire's life. I hadn't known Blaire.

"I did it because I loved my sister. I had no idea what his other family was going through. I didn't care, honestly. I only cared about Nan. You were the enemy. Then you walked into my house and completely changed my world. I always swore I'd never feel guilty for breaking up that family. After all, they had broken up Nan's. Every moment I was with you, the guilt at what I'd done started to eat me alive. Seeing your eyes when you told me about your sister and your mom, God, I swear you ripped my heart out that night, Blaire. I will never get over that."

I moved over to her, and she let me get closer.

"I swear to you that as much as I love my sister, if I could go back and change things, I would. I would *never* have gone to see your dad. Ever. I'm so sorry, Blaire. I'm so fucking sorry." Tears were blurring my vision. I had to get her to understand.

"I can't tell you that I forgive you," she said softly. "But I can tell you that I understand why you did what you did. It altered my world. That can never be changed."

A tear escaped and rolled down my face. I didn't move to wipe it away. I wasn't sure when I had cried last. I had been a kid. It was something I wasn't used to anymore. But right now, I couldn't keep it in. The pain was overwhelming. "I don't want to lose you. I'm in love with you, Blaire. I've never wanted anything or anyone the way I want you. I can't imagine my world now without you in it."

"I can't love you, Rush," she said.

I let the sob I had been trying so hard to hold in break free, and my head fell into her lap. Nothing mattered. Nothing. Not anymore. I loved her completely, but I hadn't been able to win her love in return, and without it, I would never get her back. I had lost. How would I live now that I had known life with Blaire? "You don't have to love me. Just don't leave me," I said, and I let the sobs shake my body and buried my face in her leg. Had I ever felt so broken? No. And I never would again. Nothing could compare to holding heaven and losing it.

"Rush." Her voice sounded pained.

I lifted my head from her lap. She stood up and began unsnapping her shirt. I sat there, afraid to move, as she slowly began taking off her clothing, removing each piece carefully and with purpose. I didn't understand, but I was afraid to speak. If she was changing her mind, I didn't want to ruin it.

Once she was completely naked, she walked over and straddled my legs. Grabbing her waist, I buried my face in her stomach. I could feel my body trembling from having her this close, but I didn't know what it meant. I couldn't assume it meant that she forgave me. She had just said she could never love me.

"What are you doing, Blaire?" I asked finally.

She grabbed my shirt and tugged at it. I lifted my arms and let her pull it off. Then she sank down in my lap and grabbed my head and kissed me. That sweet, intoxicating taste that was Blaire filled me, and I sank my hands into her hair and held her to me. I was afraid she would change her mind. She didn't have to love me; I just wanted her to let me love her like this. It would be enough for me.

"Are you sure?" I asked, as she rocked against my erection. She just nodded.

I picked her up and laid her down on the bed. Then I removed my shoes and pants. When I was equally naked, I held myself over her and stared down at her. She took my breath away. "You're the most beautiful woman I've ever seen. Inside and out," I told her. Then I kissed her everywhere I could, every inch of her face, before pulling her bottom lip into my mouth.

She lifted her hips and opened her legs, but I wasn't ready yet. I didn't want to hurry this. I wanted to savor her. She was meant to be savored and cherished. She was meant to be loved and cared for. I would do that for her. Even if she didn't love me, I could make it enough for both of us.

I ran my hands down her body, memorizing every part of her. I didn't want to believe this was a good-bye. I didn't think Blaire would end it this way. But the fear was there, and I couldn't get enough of her. "I love you so damn much," I told her, and I lowered my head to kiss her stomach.

Her legs opened wider. I glanced up at her, knowing that I had to ask this time. She wasn't promising us a tomorrow.

"Do I need to wear a condom?" I asked, moving back up her body.

She nodded, and I felt what was left of my heart crack even more. She was putting a barrier between us. I reached for my jeans and got the condom out of my wallet, then slid it on. Blaire's eyes were on me. My cock twitched from her attention.

I ran my hands up the insides of her thighs. No one had ever been here but me. No one had touched her but me. "This will always be mine," I said, wanting to mark her permanently. I lowered myself until the tip of my erection nudged inside her. "Never been this good. Nothing has ever been this good." I swore, then filled her in one hard thrust. She wrapped her legs around me and cried out. My battered heart beat wildly against my chest. This was home. Blaire was my home. I hadn't realized how alone I was until she came into my life. I moved inside her slowly, not taking my eyes off her face. I wanted to see her eyes as I made love to her. That was what this was for me. I was making love to her body. This wasn't a fuck. This was me showing her how much she owned me.

She slipped her legs higher on me and wrapped her arms around my neck.

"I will always love you. No one will ever compare. You own me, Blaire. My heart and soul are yours," I told her as I rocked inside of her. I brushed a kiss against her lips. "Only you," I promised her. It would always only be her. She was my life now.

Our gazes locked, and she cried out. Her orgasm squeezed me tightly, sending me spiraling off after her. When the pleasure slowly faded, I looked at her, and I knew. Her eyes were telling me what I had feared. This had been her good-bye.

"Don't do this, Blaire," I pleaded.

"Good-bye, Rush," she whispered.

I refused to accept it. I couldn't let her do this. "No. Don't you do this to us."

She let her legs fall away from my body and go limp. Then she dropped her hands to her sides and turned her face away from me. "I didn't get a good-bye with my sister or my mom. Those were final good-byes I never got. This final good-bye I needed. This one time between us with no lies." The hollowness in her voice sliced me open.

I grabbed the sheets under my hands. "No. No. Please, don't," I begged.

She continued to look away from me and lay limply beneath me. How could I fight for someone who didn't want me? Someone who hated me? I had no chance of winning. I had done everything I knew how to do. But she didn't want me. Not now.

I pulled out of her and reached for my clothing. I disposed of the condom, then numbly went through the motions of putting my clothes on. She wanted me to leave. And I was just supposed to walk out of this room and leave her. How the fuck could I?

When I was dressed, I turned to look at her. She sat up, pulling her knees up to her chin to cover her nudity.

"I can't make you forgive me. I don't deserve your forgiveness. I can't change the past. All I can do is give you what you want. If this is what you want, I'll walk away, Blaire. It'll kill me, but I'll do it." I would do the only thing I could do: give her what she wanted.

"Good-bye, Rush," she repeated, and she dropped her gaze from me.

I would leave my heart here. My soul, too. She owned them. I was empty without her. I would never be the same. Blaire Wynn had changed me. She had shown me that I could love with an all-consuming love and get nothing in return. I would never love again. She was the one. She was it for me. With one final look at the woman I loved, I turned and left the room, closing the door behind me.

When I stepped out into the night, I let the rest of my tears fall.

Loving someone you don't deserve isn't easy. It hurts like hell. But not one moment of my time with Blaire would I regret.

Acknowledgments

When I wrote *Fallen Too Far*, I never imagined it would be the beginning of such a popular series. Going back and revisiting the beginning with Rush and Blaire was so much fun for me. I tried very hard to give readers new scenes and moments they missed in *Fallen Too Far*. I loved getting into Rush's head in this book. I hope it makes all you Rush Crushers happy.

I need to start by thanking my agent, Jane Dystel, who is beyond brilliant. The moment I signed with her was one of the smartest things I've ever done. Thank you, Jane, for helping me navigate through the waters of the publishing world. You are truly a badass.

The brilliant Jhanteigh Kupihea. I couldn't ask for a better editor. She is always positive and working to make my books the best they can be. Thank you, Jhanteigh, for making my new life with Atria one I am happy to be a part of. The rest of the Atria team: Judith Curr for giving me and my books a chance. Ariele Fredman and Valerie Vennix for always finding the best marketing ideas and being as awesome as they are brilliant.

The friends who listen to me and understand me the way no one else in my life can: Colleen Hoover, Jamie McGuire, and Tammara Webber. You three have listened to me and supported me more than anyone I know. Thanks for everything.

Getting Rush "right" in this book was so important to me. Having two beta readers who loved Rush and who I thought "knew" him were very important: Autumn Hull spent endless hours helping me search for the right cover model for Rush and cheered me on as I brought Rush's story to life. Natasha Tomic is the creator of the "Rush Crush" slogan and the "Peanut Butter Scene" reference. So I felt like she knew him as well as I did. Thank you, girls, for your support. Always!

Last but certainly not least:

My family. Without their support I wouldn't be here. My husband, Keith, makes sure I have my coffee and that the kids are all taken care of when I need to lock myself away and meet a deadline. My three kids are so understanding, although once I walk out of that writing cave they expect my full attention, and they get it. My parents, who have supported me all along. Even when I decided to write steamier stuff. My friends, who don't hate me because I can't spend time with them for weeks at a time because my writing is taking over. They are my ultimate support group and I love them dearly.

My readers. I never expected to have so many of you. Thank you for reading my books. For loving them and telling others about them. Without you I wouldn't be here. It's that simple.